TWISTED VIOLET

JESSA HALLIWELL

CONTENT & TRIGGER WARNING

While *Twisted Violet* is categorized as a dark romance, I consider it more of a heartfelt romance set in a really dark world. With that said, some of the content in this story is still very dark, so please read responsibly.

- **Copious Pining** - Lots of lingering looks & accidental hand brushes.
- **Death/Murder** - Don't worry, none of the main characters die.
- **Dog Content** - Yes, he lives. Yes, he's spoiled.
- **Excessive Shirtlessness** - At home? Shirtless. Training? Shirtless. FMC is in danger? You guessed it… shirtless.
- **Gratuitous Groveling** - Making their hearts and their wallets hurt.
- **Group Activities** - Sorry, mom.
- **Intimidation, Stalking, and Threats** - By the villain… gross.
- **Light Stalking** - By one of her hot bodyguards… yay.
- **Kidnapping & Captivity** - References to the FMC's past abduction and imprisonment.
- **K-Pop Demon Hunters Spoilers** - Sorry, I'm obsessed.

- **Parental Neglect & Child Abuse** - References to the FMC's rough childhood.
- **Possessive Men** - Territorial behavior disguised as "safety."
- **PTSD & Trauma Responses** - Flashbacks, disassociation, night terrors, panic attacks.
- **Sexual Assault** - Past abuse is referenced. No ultra graphic depictions.
- **Violence/Torture** - Physical fights, gun fights, self-defense killings, and rough handling/torture all performed on people who deserve it.

*For anyone who's ever looked at
three dangerously hot men and thought,
I can fix them...*

or at the very least, keep them busy.

PLAYLIST

The Happiest Girl by BLACKPINK
Feels Like by Gracie Abrams
Take You Down by ILLENIUM
Damocles by Sleep Token
Free by Rumi and Jinu (EJAE & Andrew Choi)
Happiness is a butterfly by Lana Del Rey
Moonstruck by ENHYPEN
this is me trying by Taylor Swift
Sorry, I Love You by Stray Kids
Those Eyes by New West
ur so pretty by Wasia Project
Zombie by YUNGBLUD
Break My Heart Again by FINNEAS
Pretty Boy by The Neighborhood
Listen to it on Spotify

PROLOGUE

VIOLET

I was nine when I realized there was something wrong with me.

Intense. I know. But growing up in the house I did meant learning things way earlier than any child should.

I don't remember a lot about that day, but I do remember it being early, because the dense fog that normally blanketed the city had yet to lift, and the world outside was still coated in a soft milky haze.

After waiting by my bedroom window for what felt like hours, my mother's gold sedan had finally appeared in our driveway, and I knew I only had a few precious moments to catch her before she inevitably slipped out again.

Normally, I paid little attention to my mother's comings and goings. She wasn't home very often, and when she was, my older sister, Stevie, and I were usually the last things on her mind.

But that day, I needed her. My class had a field trip to the planetarium, and my teacher, Mrs. Miller, made it clear that I couldn't go without a parent's signature. My father was just as unreliable as my mother, so staying up and waiting for one of them to show was my only real option.

I should've known there was something off with my mother the moment I came downstairs and saw her sitting at the kitchen table. Her face was tight, and she had a glazed-over look in her eyes that raised the fine hairs on the back of my neck.

I didn't know she was an addict back then. All I knew was she seemed out of it a lot and wasn't always the best at noticing me. But she was my mom, and I needed her, so I ignored the uneasy feeling in my gut and carefully stepped towards her.

"Mom, could you sign this?" I asked gently, setting the permission slip and pen down on the table in front of her.

She didn't respond and continued to glare at her freshly poured bowl of cereal.

"Mom?" I tried again, holding my breath as I moved in closer to tap her on the shoulder.

I hated the way she smelled. Like a pungent mixture of sugar and burnt plastic. She didn't always smell like that, but over time it became the only scent I associated with her.

I tapped her again.

"Mom?"

"Leave me the hell alone." She hissed, turning her head to pin me with a vicious glare. "Can't you see I'm busy?"

"Y- yes…" I stammered, breaking eye contact and staring down at her hands, "but I- I waited up for you. I have a field trip today."

She flexed her fingers, and the sores on them started to bleed. There were more of them now. Way more than the last time I saw her. Stevie always told me it was rude to stare, but I couldn't pull my eyes away from them. They looked so painful.

"Of course you need something." She glowered, shoveling a heaping spoonful of O's into her mouth. "Why else would you come looking for Mommy Dearest? It's not like you actually give a fuck about me."

I looked up at her with wide eyes and shook my head. "That's not true-"

"Bullshit." She snapped, cutting me off as little bits of cereal and milk flew from her mouth. "All you and your sister do is take. Take. Take. Take. Like greedy little vultures. Well, I've news for you, sweetheart. Sometimes, life doesn't go your way. Sometimes, you don't get what you want. And tonight is one of those nights. Now kindly fuck off and let me eat in peace."

I should've left. I should've gone back up to my room and not pushed any further. But I needed her. I needed her to see me, to care, to love me in a way that only a mother could.

"Mom, please... just sign it. I promise I won't ask you for anything else."

She narrowed her eyes and glared at me like I was a filthy wad of bubblegum stuck to her shoe. "Did you not hear what the fuck I said?" She snapped, ripping her cereal bowl off the table and chucking it towards the wall behind me at full force.

Soggy cereal and jagged pieces of her bowl went flying everywhere. Splattering me with sticky sweet milk and scratching the back of my arms and legs with little fragments of cheap ceramic.

"God," she muttered, running a hand through her dark tangled hair, "haven't you realized no one wants to deal with you? Not me. Not your father. Not even your fucking sister! She's just too much of a coward to tell you."

"Th- that's not true." I whispered, my voice breaking as tears welled in my eyes. "Stevie loves me. She's the one who takes care of me."

"That's because she feels sorry for you." She laughed.

"Don't be stupid, Alexandra. Pity isn't love. People will feel sorry for someone weak and pathetic like you. But they'll never love them."

I stood there, my feet frozen in place, as her bitter words sliced me in two.

Was she right?

Did Stevie really feel sorry for me?

I mean, we were half-sisters, but apart from that, she and I didn't really have much in common. She was strong, and she never really let anything affect her. I was weak and would cry over the smallest things.

How could someone like her ever really love someone like me?

I stared at my mother. Really stared at her, and for the first time in my life, I realized I hated her. I hated that she was never good to me. I hated that she cared more about herself than she ever did about me. But more than anything, I hated that deep down I knew she was right.

Pity isn't love. It may sometimes feel like love. It may have all the markings of love. But it isn't the same, and it never will be.

I walked out of the kitchen without another word. I could feel the hot tears coming, and I didn't want to give her the satisfaction of knowing she had made me cry.

"Oh, and Alexandra?" She added, catching me just before I walked up the stairs. "Take this with you." She said, crumpling the permission slip and throwing it at me. "You aren't going anywhere, and in the morning, your ass better clean this shit up."

I raced up the stairs without looking back. I hated that I was being a coward, but once I was sure I was out of earshot, the tears just wouldn't stop, no matter how hard I tried. What she did hurt me, but what she said hurt even worse.

It's been years since she spewed those venomous words, and though she's long-since passed away, everything she said to me that night still weighs heavy on my heart.

I wish I could say I grew up and ended up proving her wrong. That after graduating high school, I went out into the world, stood strong on my own, and made something of myself. But in the end, I became exactly who she knew I would be. Weak. Needy. And tragically unlovable.

ONE

VIOLET

I can't sleep.

It's not that I'm not tired. I *am*. Exhausted actually. My body aches in places I didn't even know existed, but my mind won't stop racing.

I've spent the last three days running on fumes, sitting at my sister's bedside, watching her fight for her life. Between the constant beeps of machinery, the sterile smell of the hospital, and the muffled voices in the hall, it was nearly impossible to sleep. But the main thing that kept me awake was fear. Fear that I might wake up to a world where she's gone.

Now I'm back at the safe house. Lying in a bed that's too soft, in a room that's too quiet, and all I can think about is how it feels like she's already gone.

I roll over and stare at the ceiling.

I didn't want to leave the hospital. Dallas, Niko, and Rome spoke with Stevie's guys, and the decision was made for me. I told them I wanted to stay, but they insisted.

They said I needed rest, that I could come back as soon as I got some sleep, but I know what they really meant. They didn't think I could handle it anymore. They saw how fragile I was, how close I was to breaking, and decided to get me out of there.

The shitty thing is, I can't even be mad at them, they're *right*.

I'm not strong enough to handle this. I never have been.

Stevie slit her own throat to save everyone, to save *me*, and I just stood there. Frozen and useless, watching her bleed.

I forced her to let me go with them that night. In some pathetic attempt to prove I could handle it. To show that I wasn't just this thing that always has to be protected.

If I had listened to her, maybe things would've played out differently. Maybe she wouldn't be lying in that hospital bed right now, barely holding on.

God.

What if she doesn't wake up?

I try to push the thought away, but it clings to me and grows.

What if she's already gone?

I roll over onto my stomach and let out a scream into my pillow.

"V?" A soft voice calls out, sounding hesitant. "Everything okay?"

Dallas.

The southern drawl in his rich voice usually puts a smile on my face. Not tonight, though. Tonight, there's nothing to smile about.

"I'm fine." I say, forcing the words past the lump in my throat.

"Any news?" His question is gentle, but the words hit me harder than I expect.

"Nothing yet." I whisper.

He stays quiet for a moment, but I feel him there, standing still in the doorway behind me. Like he's terrified one wrong move will make me unravel.

"You should eat something," he says quietly. "You haven't had an actual meal in days."

I shake my head without looking up at him. "I'm not hungry."

He steps closer, and I feel his presence fill the room.

I know he's just trying to help, but I don't want him in here. *I don't want anyone in here.* I just want to be alone with my thoughts and my guilt, and I want to freaking drown in them.

"V, you have to take care of yourself." He says, laying a gentle hand on my shoulder. "Stevie wouldn't want you-"

"Don't do that." I say, shrugging his hand off my shoulder as I turn to face him. "Don't try to tell me what my sister would want. You barely know her. You barely know me."

Hurt flashes in his warm brown eyes, and his jaw tightens.

"I'm just trying to look out for you." He says, his voice quieter now, and sounding a little strained.

I stare at the wall behind him, too tired to take the sting out of my words. "I get that this is your job, but I'm fine, Dallas. So please, just leave me alone. If anyone asks, I'll say you got me to eat something. Okay? Stand down soldier, your mission's accomplished."

He holds my gaze for a moment and opens his mouth, as if he's about to say something, but at the last second he stops himself and takes a step back like he's trying to distance himself from whatever line I just drew between us.

"I'll leave you alone." He says, turning to leave.

The door clicks shut behind him, and the silence that follows feels even heavier than it did before.

———

I LAY THERE FOR A WHILE, just staring out the open window, trying not to fall apart.

The curtains shift with the breeze, revealing glimpses of

the night sky and the redwoods surrounding the property, but I'm not really seeing any of it. Just zoning out and letting my mind go blank. Then something moves across my line of sight. *Fast.* A shape or a shadow. Gone before I can fully register it.

I sit up slowly and keep my eyes locked on the window.

It's probably nothing, I think to myself, *a bird or a branch, or my imagination being cruel again.*

Still, I slide out of bed and cross the room to check.

Reaching for the curtain, I curl my fingers tightly around the fabric, and quickly jerk it back. *Nothing.* Just an empty yard and a few branches swaying in the breeze.

I stand there for a second, starting to question my own sanity.

Did I imagine it?

My mind does that now, plays tricks on me. It turns breezes into footsteps and shadows into monsters. It's like my body doesn't know how to feel safe anymore, so it's constantly creating imaginary threats.

I close the window, lock it, and draw the blackout curtains tight. Just in case. Then I crawl back into bed and slide my headphones over my ears.

The music starts, and the world fades away instantly. Silencing the creaking walls and my ridiculous intrusive thoughts and replacing it with low aching vocals that bleed into the deepest parts of me.

An hour passes, maybe two. Time blurs and stretches as I drift somewhere between restlessness and sleep.

I think about my past. About the time I spent trapped in that shed, and how I'll probably never feel safe again. I think about Stevie. About what she did for me, and how I'll never forgive myself if she dies. I think about Dallas, too. About the way he looked like he genuinely cared, and the way I shut him out anyway.

God, what's wrong with me?

Why can't I seem to do anything right?

The darkness in the room shifts, and a sliver of light appears on the wall across from me. It doesn't move at first. It just lingers there for a moment. Then it widens, and I see a flicker of shadow cross it, before it narrows and disappears again.

Someone sets something on the nightstand behind me. A plate of food, most likely. I catch the scent of bacon and something sweet in the air. I don't turn around to thank them. I just lie there, still as stone, pretending to be asleep.

I'm sure it's Dallas, and honestly, after what happened earlier, I'm too much of a coward to face him right now.

Dallas is always there for me, breaking up my dark thoughts with a flirty grin or stupid joke. He hides behind all that pretty boy charm, but I can tell his heart is too big for his own good. He has this innate ability to show up for me when things get heavy and find a way to carry some of the weight, even if I never ask him to.

I can't believe I tore into him like he was the enemy.

I feel him shift behind me, like he's about to leave, and something in me twists. Before my ego can intervene, my hand shoots out, bridging the gap between us as my fingers close around his warm arm.

"I'm not ready to talk," I say, my voice barely above a whisper. "But will you stay and hold me? Just for a little while?"

For a moment, I'm not sure if he answers, but then I feel the bed shifts behind me as the mattress dips under his weight. His large body folds around mine, as he drapes one arm over my waist, and slips the other under the pillow beneath my head. And then, without any hesitation, he holds me.

No words or pressure. Only quiet, steady warmth.

Something in me fractures at the feel of his touch, and the first sob escapes before I can stop it. It rips from a place so deep, so suppressed, that it almost hurts as it forces its way out.

I curl tighter into myself as the tears spill fast, soaking the pillow beneath me. My hand finds his across my stomach, and I clutch it hard, clinging to it like it's the only thing keeping me tethered to the world right now.

I don't allow myself to cry anymore. I don't allow myself to need anything. But in his arms, it doesn't feel shameful or weak. It feels *safe.*

I close my eyes and release a slow, steady breath.

I'm okay. I'm okay. I'm okay.

Dallas shifts closer as my breathing evens, and before I even realize what he's doing, his lips are on me. He presses a soft kiss to the back of my neck, and every ounce of safety and comfort that was once between us shatters.

My eyes flare in dark, and my body tenses immediately.

That's not why I asked him to stay. Maybe I sent the wrong message without even realizing it? God. Of course I did. I asked him to get into bed with me. Why wouldn't he think I wanted more?

I go quiet, and everything inside me stills, as I watch the scene play out from outside my body. Tears well in my eyes, and a lump forms in my throat. For a second, I think I might actually cry, but crying never made the pain stop. Not when it mattered. But giving people what they wanted? *That did.*

I swallow the lump in my throat and force myself to reach back for his waistband.

If this is what he came for…

If this is what it costs to feel cared for, then that's the price I'll pay.

I've done worse for a lot less.

But then, his heavy hand wraps around my wrist and stops me. *Gently.* And he carefully threads his fingers through mine instead.

There's no pressure in his touch, no hidden expectations.

He's making it clear he's just here to hold me, and it absolutely wrecks me because no one has ever done that before.

The tears hit again, harder this time. My chest shakes, and my throat burns, and I can't shake the feeling that this is what real safety feels like. What real kindness feels like. What love might look like, if I ever deserved it.

Eventually, the tears slow, my breathing evens, and for the first time in days, maybe longer, I start to drift. Not into nightmares, not into panic, but into sleep, wrapped in arms that make me feel safe.

I want so badly to hold on to this feeling. To bottle it and guard it forever. But deep down, I know it won't last. Nothing good ever does.

TWO

ROME

The plate in my hand is still warm.

Piled high with a bunch of sugary shit she loves so much. French toast, orange juice, and a double chocolate chip muffin that's close to the size of her head. She hates eggs, so the only protein on the plate is two strips of bacon, and even that barely qualifies considering it's mostly composed of grease and salt.

How this girl has managed to survive on carbs alone is a fucking mystery to me, but if tempting her with this crap is the only way to get her to eat something, then so be it.

Dallas tried to get her to eat a couple of hours ago, but that blew up in his face spectacularly, and he ended up storming off to "get some air". Now it's my turn and, unlike my much more good-natured best friend, I'm not going to let her bratty attitude stop me from getting the job done.

I knock once. No answer. *Figures.*

I turn the handle and nudge the door open with my foot, without waiting for permission. It's a dick move, but she gave up privacy the second she decided to stop eating.

The room's darker than it was earlier. The heavy curtains are drawn, and I can barely make out her silhouette on the other side of the room. She's lying on the bed, facing away from me with headphones on, and pillows surrounding her.

I take two steps inside and close the door behind me.

"Get up." I order, my voice flat and clipped.

She ignores me and keeps staring at the wall, like I'm not even here. *Fucking ridiculous.*

She's obviously still pissed we dragged her out of the hospital. Sulking because we made a call she didn't agree with, even if it was for her benefit.

I roll my eyes and take another step toward the bed, already running through the speech I'm gonna have to give. Something short and to the point about how we're not her enemies, how we didn't do it to hurt her, and how this isn't personal. But then I see it. The tremble in her shoulders, and everything in me stills.

She's not sulking. Not pouting. Not staging a silent protest. She's *mourning*. And I feel like a fucking idiot. She doesn't need food. She needs her world back.

This sad little pile of sugar and grease won't fix whatever is going on inside her head, and it definitely won't erase the image of her sister lying in that hospital bed.

I stand there staring at her back, thinking how fucked it is that all I have to offer her is this plate. Not that it even matters, not that she'd expect anything more from me. It's not like Violet and I are friends.

She's bratty, impulsive, too trusting for her own good. She calls me bossy, says I've got control issues, and jokes that I probably alphabetize my socks.

Hell, she won't even turn to look at me, and I'll admit, that concerns me more than it should.

I set the plate down on the nightstand, careful not to let it clatter. It's stupid how quiet I'm trying to be. Acting as if any noise might rip whatever thin thread is holding her together.

I take a step back, my mind already halfway out the door, but then she shifts and blindly reaches her hand back for me. Her fingers wrap around my wrist, soft but certain.

"I'm not ready to talk," she says, her voice small as she still faces the wall. "But will you stay and hold me? Just for a little while?"

I freeze.

This is a line. One I promised myself I wouldn't cross. I was hired to bring her home and keep her safe. Not to crawl into bed with her like some opportunistic asshole.

But there's a part of me, a quiet, insistent part, that wants to say yes before she even finishes the sentence. It's the same part of me that gravitated towards her the moment we found her in that shed.

She was sitting in the corner with her knees pulled to her chest and her hair caked with blood. She was bruised, barely conscious, and yet somehow, still so fucking alive. I moved closer, and her wild green eyes locked onto mine, as if she was sizing me up.

She didn't cry, didn't speak. She just stared and something in that look on her face wrecked me.Because she didn't look like a victim. She looked like someone who refused to die.

Even after everything her trafficker did to her, she was still in there. Quiet, shaken, but not gone, and I admired the hell out of her for that.

But she was a job, so I buried my feelings. Pretended they didn't exist. Now, with her holding my wrist like I'm her fucking lifeline, that feeling is coming back, and it's impossible to ignore.

Getting close to her is a mistake. But it's one I'm going to make anyway.

I EASE FORWARD and climb into bed behind her. The mattress dips beneath me, the blanket pulling just slightly as I settle in. She doesn't look at me, just keeps her face buried in the pillows like she's trying to stay hidden. I slide one arm beneath her pillow, the other over her waist, and I hold her. My touch isn't tight or tender, it's steady. I'm simply giving her something to lean on without making a thing of it.

She exhales and I feel her start to soften. Not a lot, but enough to know she needed this. Needed *me*. Even if I am the last person who should be in this bed.

I'm the man who tells himself he doesn't care, doesn't get attached, doesn't cross lines. Except I do. Because right now, I'm holding her like I've wanted to from the moment she reached for me in that shed. And I can't even pretend it's about the job anymore.

I feel it when the first sob hits her. Her whole body jerks with it. She tries to muffle it, tries to be quiet, as if crying is something to be ashamed of. So I hold her even tighter.

She melts into me, and the scent of her hair hits me. Sweet and warm, like vanilla and sleep. Not a product or a perfume, just her.

I breathe it in and I don't know what the fuck comes over me. Maybe it's how fragile she feels. Maybe it's the way she trusted me, of all people, with this moment. Or maybe it's the part of me that's been starving for her since the moment I laid eyes on her. But before I can stop myself, I lean in and press a kiss to the back of her neck.

It's soft, barely there, but her whole body goes completely still.

Fuck.

I went too far. I can try to tell myself it's harmless. That it's just a quiet kiss she'll forget about in the morning. But even as I think it, I know I'm full of shit.

She didn't ask for that. She asked me to stay, to hold her,

to be someone who expected nothing in return, and I fucking blew it.

I'm an idiot.

I exhale, trying to reel it back in, trying to convince myself it doesn't matter, that I can still be what she needs. But then she shifts, and before I can process it, she's reaching for my belt.

My brain blanks for a second, and then I freeze. Because I know what this is, what she's offering. And yeah, maybe I've thought about her like that before, but not like this, not when she's still reeling from everything.

I catch her wrist gently, before she can go further, and thread our fingers together instead.

She freezes, nods her head softly, and then breaks all over again.

Her sobs return, sharper this time. *Messier.* Like stopping her hand was worse than letting it happen.

I hold her tighter, not because I have to, but because I *want* to. And for the first time since we met, I don't feel bad about that.

———

I LIE THERE FOR HOURS, staring at the wall, and listening to her breathe. Now and then, she shifts in my arms, like she's testing to see if I'm still here. I try not to think too hard about why that makes me feel something.

Eventually, a thin strip of sunlight slips through the gap in the curtains. It hits the far wall and crawls up. Slow, warm, and unwelcome.

It's morning already. She'll be up soon, and she might be hungry. I glance at the cold plate on the nightstand.

Shit.

I'd better make her something fresh.

Careful not to wake her, I untangle our hands, ease my

arm out from under her pillow and slip out of bed. She stirs a little but doesn't wake up, murmuring something unintelligible before sinking her face deeper into the pillows.

I pause for a second, just to take one last look at her, then I walk out the door.

———

THE HALLWAY'S quiet as I head for the kitchen, plate in hand. Violet's out cold, but I keep my steps light on the off chance she'll hear me.

I round the corner, and as I do, I catch the sound of something sizzling and the low murmur of conversation.

Shit.

Walking into the kitchen, I see Niko leaning against the fridge drinking a cup of coffee and Dallas at the stove, barefoot and shirtless, flipping pancakes.

They both look up when they hear me approaching.

Dallas gives me a slow, knowing grin. "Morning."

I give him a grunt and head for the trash bin to toss the scraps before heading to the sink.

Niko tips his chin toward me. "She eat any of it?"

"Not really."

Dallas flips a pancake. "How is she?"

"Fine, she slept most of the night."

They don't say anything else right away, but I can feel them watching me.

I open the fridge to grab some bacon and throw it into a hot pan.

"Did she, uh… talk to you?" Dallas asks.

I glance over at him and can see the undercurrent of hope in his eyes as he finishes plating his breakfast.

"No," I say, shaking my head. "She wasn't really in the mood to talk."

"But she asked you to stay?" Niko asks.

I glance over at him. He's not mocking me, he just looks curious.

"Yeah," I say. "Just for a bit. I think she just didn't want to be alone."

Dallas nods, as if that answers something for him.

"It's good you were there for her." Dallas says. "I'm glad she trusts you."

I grip the handle of the pan and focus on the sizzle. "Yeah. Can we be done talking about this now?"

"You're cooking for her, aren't you?" Dallas asks, smirking like he can't help himself as he plates his pancakes. "You're setting the bar kind of high, man. Next thing we know, you'll be writing her poetry."

I level him with a look. "Say one more word and I'll crack this skillet over your big-ass head."

Niko huffs a low laugh and nearly spits out his coffee.

"Hey, my head is perfectly proportioned to my body. You're the one freaking out because your heart finally did something human and now you don't know what to do with yourself."

I shove a few slices of bread into the toaster. "It did not-"

The smell of something burning hits me and I turn to find the bacon burning with thick smoke pluming off the pan.

"Fuck," I mutter, yanking the pan off the burner and tossing it into the sink.

Dallas chuckles as he walks up behind me to have a look at the aftermath. "Pretty sure she'd prefer her food not incinerated, but you do you."

I sigh. "I'll go pick something up."

"You should grab donuts. The pink ones with sprinkles are her favorite. Oh, and don't forget donut holes. For me, not for her," he adds with a wink.

I don't answer. I just grab my keys and flip him off as I head for the door.

"Proud of you, man." He calls out after me, making me pause. "For once, you didn't let the job hold you back."

I shake my head and push the door open.

The cold air hits me like a reset, but his words linger in the back of my mind. I *didn't* put the job first last night, and maybe there'll be hell to pay for that. But right now? It feels worth it. Because for a few hours...I had her.

THREE

VIOLET

I WAKE UP WARM.

That's the first thing that registers. I feel the heat of a body pressed against my back, and the weight of the thick comforter tucked tightly around me. But when I open my eyes, I'm all alone.

I sit up slowly, brushing the lavender tangles from my face, and scan the room. Dallas is gone. So is the plate of food he brought for me.

As if on cue, my stomach growls.

I shift to the edge of the bed and squint in the low light. I *really* don't want to get up right now. But at the same time, there's a weird sense of calm in my chest, like maybe I cried out just enough grief last night to function.

Go me.

I throw on an oversized hoodie and shuffle toward the kitchen like a feral raccoon looking for snacks. I don't know what I'm expecting to find, but when I turn the corner and see Dallas leaning against the counter alone, sipping coffee, I feel… uneasy.

Dallas has always been annoyingly attractive. Like the makes you roll your eyes once you realize you've been staring at him for too long, kind of attractive. With his tan skin, effortless charm, and those stupid little dimples that show up every time he smiles. But after last night, it's like I'm seeing him clearly for the first time.

He looks up as I step into the room, and his face softens. "Hey, you." He says, taking a sip of his coffee. "Sleep okay?"

"Define *okay*," I mutter, rubbing my puffy eyes.

He gives me a smirk and sets down his mug. "Well, at least you got some sleep."

"Where are the guys?"

"Niko's around here somewhere and Rome slipped out a while ago."

"Oh, okay, cool." I say, hovering awkwardly. I lean against the fridge, pretending to be casual. "I'm sorry, by the way."

His brow quirks up. "For what?"

"For last night…" I gesture vaguely toward the hallway. "I know I probably put you in a tough position."

Dallas tilts his head like he's trying to piece it together. Then his expression softens.

"Oh. That?" He waves it off. "Don't worry about it. It's fine."

I bite the inside of my cheek. "Are you sure? I was worried I might've messed things up between us."

He smiles at me, but it doesn't quite reach his eyes. "V, I'm not reading too much into what happened, and I don't think you should either. Let's just move on, yeah?"

I turn away before he can see the hit land.

"Yeah," I say lightly, opening the fridge like it's no big deal. "Sounds good to me." I pull out a bottle of water and twist the cap just to keep my hands busy.

He's trying to be kind, trying to make it easy, but all I hear is that last night didn't mean anything to him. *I thought some-*

thing shifted between us, but maybe I read it wrong. I guess I misread a lot of things last night.

I take a long sip of water to drown the ache rising in my throat.

The front door opens, and I glance over my shoulder. Rome steps into the kitchen, holding a bakery box and a drink tray like he's some kind of brooding delivery boy. All tall, dark, and emotionally repressed. His eyes land on me and linger for a second, like he's waiting for me to say something first. Then he looks away and his jaw tightens. He sets the box on the counter and pops it open.

"Brought donuts," he says, voice neutral. "Pink ones. With sprinkles."

I blink at him.

That's… *weird.*

And unexpected.

He doesn't look smug about it, either. No biting one-liner. No sarcastic jab. Which isn't like Rome… *at all.* It unsettles me more than any insult ever could.

I straighten, and raise a brow. "You brought home sugar? You hate sugar."

Dallas smiles as he catches a white pastry bag Rome tosses to him and heads out of the kitchen. Rome says nothing. Just nudges the box toward me and takes a small step back.

My heart pounds, but not in a good way. Rome is being nice. *To me* of all people. *Why?* Dallas must have told him how bad it got last night. How I fell apart in his arms and stupidly misread his signals. Now Rome is here with donuts and kind eyes, as if he needs to be delicate with me. Because he feels sorry for me.

I grab one from the box and rip a piece off with my teeth. It's warm, sweet, and way too good for this moment.

"Thanks," I say finally, not meeting his eyes. "That was… nice of you."

I force a smile, but it feels brittle on my face. "I'm feeling better now. So you totally don't have to hang around if you've got other things to do."

Rome goes still for a second, and then he nods once. "Right." He says, his jaw flexing. "Glad you're feeling better."

Rome turns and walks out. The door slams behind him, and I flinch at the sound.

A second later, I realize I'm not alone. Niko's standing in the hallway, half-shadowed, with a coffee in hand. His expression isn't sharp like Rome's or easy like Dallas'. It's unreadable. He gives me the faintest nod, then turns and walks away.

I stand there, chewing a donut I don't even want anymore, wondering what just happened and why the hell it bothers me so much.

FOUR

VIOLET

THE CALL FROM ATLAS CAME EARLY THIS MORNING. HE DIDN'T give me much detail, but what he said stuck with me. Stevie's awake. Not speaking yet, but very much alive, alert, and breathing on her own.

I didn't tell Rome, Dallas, or Niko the news. Ever since my little breakdown a few days ago, they've all been keeping their distance from me. They're trying to hide it, but I can sense the shift. I feel it in every conversation that trails off the moment I enter the room.

I've overstayed my welcome. That much is clear, and maybe it's pathetic, but I'd rather pull away now than wait for them to finally get the nerve to say it. So once I ended the call, I packed my things, called a taxi, and headed straight to the hospital.

Now I'm standing just outside of her room, trying to find the courage to walk in.

She's in there. I can see her through the window. She's propped up slightly with her eyes open, blinking slowly like it's hard for her to stay awake. Her face is bruised, her throat is bandaged, and there's a bunch of wires sticking to her. But she's awake.

That's good. *That's everything.*

Her guys are all stationed around her room like personal guard dogs. Cyrus is holding her hand. Tristan is brushing her hair behind her ear. Atlas is speaking with her nurse. And Ezra is watching her heart monitor like a freaking hawk.

My stomach knots as my fingers twitch against the strap of my bag.

They look so happy. So in love. Like they've lived a hundred lifetimes together and would still choose her in the next.

I shift my weight and the strap of my bag bites into my shoulder.

God, I don't want to intrude. This feels like a moment that belongs to them. Something sacred and hard-won. I should come back later. Besides, watching them orbit around her like she's gravity itself is hard enough to watch out here. I can't imagine what it'd be like to see it up close.

I'm happy for my sister. *Of course* I am. But seeing them together is also a reminder of everything I'll never have. I've already accepted that love like that isn't made for someone like me, but that doesn't stop it from stinging a little every time I see it.

I turn to leave, and just as I'm about to walk away, Stevie spots me and gestures for me to come in.

I set my bag on the floor and step inside before I can talk myself out of it. I approach her bedside, and she grabs my hand and gives it a weak squeeze. She doesn't say anything, but it's like I can feel what she's thinking.

She's okay.

We're okay.

Everyone is okay.

I sit there for hours with her, not saying much. Most of the time, I just hold her hand and try not to cry. I want to say thank you. I want to say I'm sorry, but none of the words will come out.

Eventually, a team of nurses comes in to check her vitals, so I step out of the room to give them space, and Atlas follows behind me.

"Hey," he says gently, keeping his eyes on Stevie through the window, "You doing okay?"

I nod. "What are the doctors saying?"

"She's okay. She'll heal."

I glance at her. "Good."

He tilts his head and eyes the duffel bag I left out by the door. "What's in the bag?"

Embarrassment warms my cheeks. "Yeah, um, about that. I was wondering if-"

"The guest house is yours." He says, cutting me off.

I furrow my brow. "Wait… what?"

"It has been since the minute we learned about you," he says simply. "Move in. Stevie would want that. So would we."

I blink, thrown by the certainty in his voice. "Are you sure?"

He takes his eyes off Stevie to meet mine. "You're family. Stay as long as you like. Stay forever if you want."

My throat tightens. "Thanks," I murmur. "I, um… I guess I'll swing by later to drop off my stuff."

"Might as well go now." He says with a shrug. "The nurses are going to take her in for more testing in a few minutes. Here," he says, pulling out his keys and tossing them at me, "take my car."

I stare at him, a little dumbfounded. *Just like that?*

"Thanks." I say, averting my gaze. "Do you guys need me to grab anything while I'm there?"

He nods. "I've got a bag packed for Stevie. A black leather duffle sitting in the foyer by the stairs. Bring it back with you?"

"Sure."

"Thanks, kid. I'll text you the gate code."

He squeezes my shoulder gently and heads back into Stevie's room without another word.

———

THE RAIN IS COMING DOWN HARD by the time I reach the gates at the edge of The Reapers' estate. The headlights cut through the downpour in hazy beams, lighting up the massive black iron bars ahead. Rain lashes across the windshield in wild streaks, blurring the stone pillars and the ivy-cloaked walls.

I put the car in park, leave the engine running, and just sit there for a second. The gate doesn't move. No lights flash. No click of an automatic unlock. Only the sound of rain hammering the roof, and the faint hiss of the heater.

Oh right.

Atlas sent me the code.

I reach for my phone and spot the keypad box mounted to a post right beside me. It's one of those sleek metal boxes fitted with a security camera and recessed buttons. I've never actually used one before, but it shouldn't be too difficult.

I roll down the window and lean toward the keypad, holding my phone in one hand, while the other hovers over the buttons. The rain hits immediately, slicing across my arm and dripping down the inside of my sleeve. The metal keys are slick, and my fingers are shaking from the cold.

I punch in the first number, then the second. My thumb slips on the third. The red light flashes. *Denied.*

I suck in a breath and wipe my hand on my jeans. The rain is pounding now, slapping me in the face like it's personal. My hoodie's soaked up to my shoulder, and my hair's already sticking to my face.

I tap the panel again, slower this time, pressing hard, trying to make it register. But the buttons are slippery and cold. The ridges barely give under pressure, and I can't tell if I've hit the right number or if the damn thing's just ignoring me.

I squint at the blurry little LED above the pad, and water streams into my eyes. The red light flashes, and it feels like it's mocking me. I drop my forehead against the steering wheel.

"Okay," I whisper. "Fine."

I throw the car in park, shove the door open, and step into the downpour. The air hits me like ice. Soaking my clothes in seconds, and my boots sink into the muddy gravel. Something shifts in the hedge. A rustle maybe. Or wind. But the rain's so loud I can't tell the difference anymore.

I pull my hood tighter and trudge to the keypad, shielding my phone with one hand while I try to press the numbers with the other. My thumb hesitates on the fourth digit. The light flashes green. *Finally.*

I let out a breath and step back, shoulders sagging as I slip my phone back into my pocket. And then, something moves behind me.

A crunch of gravel. That's all the warning I get before something crashes into me. I'm pushed so hard my boots skid on the mud and my breath flies out of me in a sharp, ugly gasp. The keypad light blinks uselessly in front of me as a man's arm snakes around my neck and drags me backward into the shadows between the stone wall and the hedges lining the drive.

I scream, but it's useless. It's drowned out by the rain and muffled by his hand over my mouth.

"Quiet," he growls into my ear, his breath hot and sour. "Don't make this harder than it has to be."

I kick. Slam my elbow back. Nothing works. His grip is like steel, and the rain's so loud now I can barely hear myself think, let alone fight.

He jerks me harder, nearly lifting me off the ground before

slamming me hard against the keypad post. My head hits the metal, and stars explode behind my eyes.

"You stupid bitch," he snarls, "He'll have my head for that."

Panic tears through me. He's going to take me. He's going to bring me back to *him*.

No.

NO, NO, NO.

I claw at his arm, nails digging into skin and drawing blood. He grunts and jerks back, just enough to loosen his grip, then shoves me off of him.

I stumble, hit the gravel hard, and my hands slam into mud and rock, but my momentum carries me, and I roll, slamming shoulder-first into the front fender of Atlas's car.

My face lands just beneath the edge of the open driver's door. That's when I see it. A glint of black beneath the seat. Tucked in tight, almost hidden. Atlas's gun.

I lunge for it. The man grabs my ankle behind me, trying to drag me back, but I twist, scrambling half-under the dashboard. My fingers close around the grip. Safety's already off.

I roll onto my back, raise the weapon with both hands, and fire.

Bang.

He stumbles, lets go, and grunts in pain. I scramble up to my feet and fire again.

Bang.

This time, he drops.

I hit the ground hard, knees slamming into wet gravel. The gun falls from my grip with a clatter. My stomach heaves, and a stream of vomit forces itself out.

Rain is everywhere. In my eyes, in my mouth, and soaking through all of my clothes. I can't hear anything except the pounding in my chest. My lungs are working but I can't feel the air.

I want to run, I want to scream, but I can't. I just sit there, frozen, staring at the lifeless body in horror. I don't know if he's breathing, I don't know if I hit anything that matters. I just know he's not moving, and I can't deal with this alone.

I reach for my phone with fingers that don't feel like mine and swipe blindly at the screen. It takes three tries to find his name.

Niko.

I press the call button and bring the phone to my ear. He answers on the second ring.

"Vi?" His voice is low, clipped, and alert.

Just hearing his voice on the other end makes me breathe easier. I open my mouth to answer him, but nothing comes out. Just a breath. Then another.

"Talk to me."

"Niko." My voice splinters. "I need you."

Silence on the other end.

"Where are you?"

"The gate," I whisper. "Stevie's house."

"On my way."

FIVE

NIKO

THE CALL WAS UNEXPECTED. HER NAME LIT UP MY SCREEN. No text. No warning. She didn't say much, just my name, shaky and broken, like she was barely holding herself together, and I didn't even hesitate. *Hell,* I didn't even ask what happened.

I was in my car, running red lights on the way out of the city, praying I wasn't too late.

The gates to the estate are wide open when I get there. So is the driver's side door of the car. Vi is on the ground, slumped in the gravel, shaking so hard I can hear her teeth chatter. There's blood on her hands, and a few feet away, there's a body.

Her eyes lock on mine as I step out of the car. "I think I killed him," she whispers. Her voice is hoarse, almost child-like. "I didn't mean to. He was trying to take me, and I... I found the gun and - I killed him, Niko. Oh my God, I killed him."

I walk past her without a word and kneel quickly to examine the body. Two shots to the chest. Already cold.

I pull out my gun, press it to his forehead, and pull the trigger without blinking.

Bang.

I turn back around to find her staring at his lifeless body. "Look at me." I say, searching her face.

She does, flinching like she expects to see judgment in my face.

"I killed him." I say softly. "Not you."

She stares at me like I just rewrote the rules of the world.

"I did it." I repeat. "Not you. Me."

She doesn't speak or move. Her lips tremble, and her fingers twitch as if they don't know whether to reach for me or to cover her face. So I make the choice for her.

I step forward slowly, crouch in front of her in the mud, and pick the gun up from where it's half-buried next to her. Then, I carefully reach out and wipe the blood from her hands with the sleeve of my sweatshirt.

"Come on," I say gently, not quite touching her. "We can't stay here."

She doesn't argue. She just nods. Silent and small.

I get her in the passenger seat and she shakes so hard it looks like her bones might snap in half. I crank the heat and grab a towel from the trunk, an old scratchy one I normally use to wipe down my windows.

She doesn't complain when I wrap it around her shoulders. She doesn't flinch when I buckle her seatbelt for her. She just watches me with those wide green eyes as I slip into the driver's seat.

She stares out the window the entire drive. She doesn't ask where we're going. She probably thinks I'm taking her back to the safe house to meet up with Rome and Dallas. *I'm not.*

I'm taking her to our penthouse. She'll be at peace there. Less questions. Fewer eyes.

She finally speaks when we're halfway down the winding

back road that leads to our apartment building. "I really didn't want him to die, you know," she whispers.

I don't look at her. "I know." I say. "But I did."

She's quiet for a long time. Then she asks, "Why?"

My hands tighten on the wheel.

Because my hands are already stained. Because yours shouldn't have to be. Because if he wasn't dead already, I would've killed him for touching you.

"It's my job." I say simply.

She doesn't ask where we are when I pull into the underground garage and doesn't blink when I enter the code that opens the steel security gate. She just stares down at her hands, like she's trying to forget they ever held a gun.

The cut the engine and the silence swells.

"I'm taking you upstairs," I say. "You can sleep. Shower. Burn your clothes, if you want."

She finally looks at me. "Where are we?"

"Our place."

Her brow creases. "Wait, your… actual home?"

I nod once.

"I didn't know you guys had a home."

I fight a smile.

"Not like that, I just thought with work…" she trails off. "You live here?"

"Sometimes."

She swallows. "Why'd you bring me here?"

Because no one else gets this. Because I don't want anyone seeing you like this but me. Because you're shaking like you might come apart, and for some reason, I can't fucking stand the idea of anyone else putting you back together.

"It's safe."

That's all I give her, but it's the truth. It's the only place in the world I trust. My sanctuary. And now I'm letting her in it.

The elevator opens into a quiet hallway. Minimalist. Clean. My door is on the right. With no number to identify it, just a biometric scanner. She watches me as I press my thumb to the reader.

When the door clicks open, I see her hesitate. Maybe because she's nervous. Maybe because she knows, intuitively, that this is something I don't share and yet, here I am, sharing it with her. Still she steps inside and looks around.

Floor-to-ceiling windows. Concrete walls. Matte finishes. Everything sharp, cold, and calculated. Everything except for her.

She stands there dripping in the middle of it all, towel still wrapped around her shoulders, her wet clothes clinging to her frame, and for a second the whole place feels warmer. Maybe bringing her here was as much for me as it was for her.

She stands there, still trembling, as the silence folds in around us. Then finally, she speaks.

"I'm sorry I dragged you into this." The words are quiet. Raw. "I panicked. I didn't know what else to do, and I just... I'm sorry."

I step closer and rest my hands on her shoulders. "Don't apologize."

Her arms cross over her chest as if she's trying to hold herself together. "I shot someone, Niko."

"You defended yourself."

"That doesn't make it better."

"But it's the truth."

"He's dead because of me," she whispers. "I know he was trying to hurt me, but I... I didn't want to be that person." She lets out a breath that sounds more like a sob. "But I am now, aren't I? I'm a killer. A monster."

That word lingers in the air between us, and hate how familiar her guilt feels. I need to do something, before it eats her alive.

I reach for her hands and take it as a good sign when she

doesn't pull away. "You're not a monster," I say, low and steady. "I've worked for monsters. You're not even close."

Her eyes flick up, glassy and wide.

"If you were truly like them. I wouldn't have brought you here."

She flinches, but there's no fear in her eyes, just understanding.

"That guilt you're feeling right now?" I murmur. "Monsters don't feel that. So if anyone's the monster here, it's me."

She shakes her head and swallows. "That's not-"

"Vi, you pulled the trigger to save yourself. I pulled it to punish him. I'm the one with blood on my hands, and honestly, I'd stain them again if it meant you didn't have to."

She crumples into me as her arms lock around my waist. She sobs into my chest and her whole body trembles as a wave of emotions crashes over her.

I wrap my arms around her and hold her tighter than I've ever held anything in my life. I don't let her go. Not when the shaking stops. Not when she whispers, "Thank you." Not even when her breathing calms and her grip loosens.

Letting go isn't in my nature anymore. Not when it comes to her.

SIX

VIOLET

I'VE BEEN SITTING HERE ALONE FOR THE LAST TWENTY MINUTES. I don't think they purposely left me out. When Atlas asked Niko to come in and tell my sister what happened, Rome and Dallas followed him on instinct. No one told me to stay behind, but no one asked me to come either.

So now I'm sitting in this quiet hallway, watching the second hand tick on an old wall clock.

It's fine.

They've got more important things to focus on. I'd probably just get in the way.

I pull my sleeves over my hands and curl them into my lap, trying to ignore the faint ache in my throat where the bruises are already forming. Niko gave me something dry to change into, but I'm still chilled from the inside out.

No one's said it out loud, but I can feel it. I'm the problem. *Again.* The girl who's a magnet for disaster. The one who can't even make it home without someone ending up bleeding.

Niko is in there explaining everything that happened. What he walked into. What I did. What he did. They'll want answers. They'll maybe even offer solutions. But there's no fixing what happened. A man is dead, and it's my fault.

The door clicks open, and footsteps echo down the hallway. I look up to find Niko and Dallas approaching, with Rome and Atlas walking right behind them. They're speaking in low voices, but when they reach me, the talking stops.

"Come on," Rome says. "Stevie wants to talk to you."

I stand and follow them wordlessly.

The hospital room feels smaller with everyone inside it. Stevie's sitting up, pale but alert, her throat still bandaged. Cyrus stands near the window. Ezra is standing at her side with his arms crossed, and Tristan is typing something quietly on his phone.

Rome's voice is steady as he talks. Detached, like he's reading off a police report instead of explaining how I almost got dragged into a van.

He tells them I had trouble getting the gate open. That I got out of the car to try again. That someone was waiting in the shadows. That he grabbed me and tried to drag me into the hedges.

He also tells them I fought back. That I was lucky and got to Atlas's gun in time. That I took the initial shots, and Niko finished him off.

He doesn't mention that I threw up afterward. That I couldn't stop shaking. That I didn't even know if I was still breathing until Niko showed up and reminded me how.

He keeps it simple. Clean. Just the facts. And maybe that's for the best, because if he told the story the way I remember it, if they saw how pathetic I really looked curled up on the gravel in the rain, they'd probably be having a very different conversation right now.

At one point, Rome mentions that Niko called him and Dallas to cleanup the mess, and Dallas' eyes flick to me. I keep mine on the floor.

When he finishes, Stevie gestures for Atlas to hand her a

notebook. She scribbles something and passes it to Cyrus, who reads it aloud.

"For her safety, we think it's best if Alex goes into hiding again."

The room goes still and my brow furrows. "What?"

Atlas glances at Stevie, then back at me. "It's just a safety precaution. We don't think this has anything to do with you. Someone hired that man to come after us. We need time to figure out who that someone is."

His words land like stones dropping to the pit my stomach. For a second, I think of *him*. The man who locked me away. The one who broke me piece by piece. He promised he'd always come back for me. He never knew my real name. Never knew where I came from. But still… the thought creeps in. Could it be him?

No.

I shove the thought aside before it can take root. That chapter's over. He's gone. *He has to be.*

"The hunt for him could get messy." Ezra adds. "Your sister is safe in the hospital. It only makes sense to secure you in one of our safe houses until it's done."

"I'm not doing that again." I say, flinching at how loud my voice sounds. "I'm not disappearing or living out of a suitcase. I just got my life back."

Stevie writes again.

"You almost died." Cyrus reads. "We aren't risking your safety. Not again."

I cross my arms, fingers digging into my elbows. "So locking me away again is the answer?"

"It's not like that," Tristan says gently.

But it is, or at least, it feels that way. I just escaped one cage and now they want to throw me into another.

The room goes quiet again. I can feel them trying to figure out how to convince me without making it sound like they're forcing me. Then Rome clears his throat. "She can stay at our place in the city."

What?

I turn to look at him and it takes more than a few seconds to process what he said. Not because the words don't make sense, but because they came from him. *Rome.* The same man who barely looked at me this past week. The one who acted as if my presence alone grated on him. Why would he offer that? Especially now?

"Our apartment in San Francisco has an extra guest room." He says, locking eyes with me. "You'll be safer under our roof. It isn't tied to The Reapers, so no one will look for you out there."

As the offer hangs in the air, I study all of their faces, trying to gauge how they really feel about it. Rome looks calm and controlled, but there's something unreadable flashing in his eyes. Niko gives me a soft smile. It's barely there, but it's enough to know he doesn't hate the idea. I look at Dallas, trying to search his eyes, but he won't even meet my gaze.

"You guys don't have to do that." I say, my voice quieter now. "I've overstayed my welcome in the safe house as it is, and I really don't want to get in the way."

"You won't be," Rome counters. "In fact, with our work schedule, most of the time you'll have the place to yourself.

For a split second, I feel something I haven't let myself feel in a long time. Hope. *Maybe I got it all wrong. Maybe they do actually want me around.* The idea of staying with them... not as a secret or a job, but as something real makes my chest ache.

But then the fear creeps in. *What if they're only offering because they feel bad for me?*

I can't be that girl anymore. The one people protect out of guilt or obligation. I can't live in someone else's space, constantly wondering if I'm overstaying my welcome again.

I search Dallas' face again, looking for something,

anything to make me believe this isn't charity. His jaw is tight. His hands fidget in his hoodie pocket, but he still won't look at me, and that hurts more than I want to admit.

Then, he speaks, quiet and steady. "You should stay with us," he says, voice rough. "It's the right call."

My breath catches. It's not what he says. It's how he says it. He means it. He truly wants me there.

I glance at Niko. He gives me a slight nod, and Rome hasn't looked away since he put the offer out there.

Maybe this isn't charity. Maybe, just maybe… they actually want me around. I nod, barely trusting my voice.

"Okay," I whisper. "I'll go."

SEVEN

DALLAS

IT'S BEEN THREE DAYS SINCE VIOLET WAS ATTACKED. LONG enough for things to settle, but not long enough for them to feel normal again.

She doesn't say much when I pick her up from the hospital. Not that I expect her to. She has to uproot her life again, and she probably isn't in much of a talking mood.

She's sitting next to me in the passenger seat with her forehead pressed against the window. She's not looking at me, she's not really looking at anything, she's just watching the city go by in a blur of neon lights.

I think about making a joke or saying something stupid to break the silence, but at the last second, I think better of it.

I don't know why, but things between us have changed. Maybe it's the fact that when she needed someone, she leaned on Rome. Maybe it's the fact that when she needed someone again, she called Niko.

I'm not mad. I'm glad they were there for her. But still, *it stings, just a little.*

I grip the steering wheel tighter and turn onto a narrow road lined with redwood trees.

Violet lifts her head from the window. "Where are we going?"

"Gotta pick someone up," I say, flicking on the blinker. "Won't take long."

She blinks at me, a little guarded, like she's not sure if she should be worried, but then the sign comes into view.

"Wagging Tails Boarding & Daycare."

She twists in her seat to face me, brow raised. "You have a dog?"

I glance at her. "You sound surprised."

Her eyes widen. "I just… didn't know. You never mentioned it."

I shrug. "I get him boarded while we're on jobs."

She fights a smile. "I *love* dogs."

Something about the way she says it makes my chest tighten. She sounds like she's admitting a secret. Something she thinks is too fragile to say out loud.

"He's a German Shepherd mix," I say, pulling into the small gravel lot in front of the pet boarding facility. "His name is Ollie. He's about 10 months old, and he's a freaking menace, which is why he can't come on missions with me."

I throw the car into park and turn off the engine. "Come meet him?"

She hesitates for a beat, double-checking our surroundings, then unbuckles and follows me out of the truck.

The moment we step inside the building, Ollie loses his mind. I barely get to the counter before he's trying to leap over it to get to me.

"Jesus, Olls," I mutter, unclipping his leash from the tech. "You're gonna break your neck."

As soon as he's free, he barrels into me, tongue out, paws everywhere, like he has no idea he weighs 50 pounds. Then he sees Violet.

She kneels instinctively with her hand out, and Ollie goes straight to her, nudging his nose under her hand and licking her palm like he's known her forever.

"Oh, my God. He's so cute." She says as Ollie jumps up and starts licking her face. "You didn't tell me he was so lovey."

"I was trying to make him look tough." I joke, ruffling Ollie's ears. "But he's ruining it."

She smiles at me. Not a half-smile. A real one. And God help me, I feel it like a punch to the ribs. That's the moment I realize how screwed I really am.

Watching her with him makes me want things I have no business wanting. Like more moments like this, like her staying, like her choosing *me*. But I don't say any of that. Instead, I open the door and lead the three of us back to the truck in silence.

As soon as we're all in, Ollie curls up in the backseat and plops his head on her shoulder, looking like it's the most natural thing in the world for him. V reaches back to scratch behind his ears, and he melts like putty in her hands.

"How long have you had him?" She asks.

"About eight months. I found him while out on a job. He was half-starved and mean as hell, but I couldn't leave him behind."

She nods slowly, still petting him.

"That's sweet."

I shrug like it's nothing, but it's not nothing. Ollie's the only thing in my life I've never second-guessed loving. And now she's here, in the passenger seat, petting him like they've known each other for years. Maybe… she could belong here too.

We don't talk much the rest of the ride, but I catch her glancing at me once, and when our eyes meet, she doesn't look away.

She just gives me the tiniest smile. And a stupid thought creeps into my mind that I can't shake. I'd do anything for that smile.

EIGHT

VIOLET

I'VE BEEN HERE BEFORE. BUT LAST TIME, I WASN'T REALLY IN THE right headspace to pay attention. Not to the floor, or the layout, or the sheer size of the place. I was half-frozen, covered in blood and rainwater, too numb to notice anything beyond the pounding in my chest.

Now, with Dallas and Ollie standing guard beside me as the elevator ascends, I take in all the details.

The design is stunning. Dark wood floors. Matte black finishes. Soft white lights glowing against the baseboards. It's the kind of simplicity money buys. Not the cold, empty kind, but the curated kind. Intentional and comfortable.

We step out of the elevator, and my feet slow automatically in front of the first door on the right.

The door is instantly familiar. So is the biometric scanner on the wall beside it. I remember leaning against it the other night, soaked and shaking, with Niko's towel draped over my shoulders.

I hesitate, my fingers brushing the edge of the frame.

Dallas glances back and raises a brow. "What're you doing?"

"Isn't this… your place?" I ask quietly.

He tilts his head. "That's Niko's wing."

It takes a second to process what he just said. "Wing?"

"Yeah." He nods down the hall. "Come on. Keep walking."

I follow, and as we round the corner, everything opens up.

The hallway branches into three more corridors, each marked subtly with a different colored door beneath the archways. The main living space stretches out in the middle, and my gaze flicks past the open-concept kitchen to the floor-to-ceiling windows. The city sprawls beyond them, rain still glistening on the glass.

This isn't just one apartment. This is the entire top floor. Rome must have a wing. Dallas too. And now, I guess I do too.

Dallas watches my reaction without saying a word, but I know he sees it on my face. The surprise. The awe. The way I'm trying to make sense of how I ended up in a place like this, surrounded by people like them. People who get bloody doing the jobs no one else will do and still come home to something this solid.

Dallas leads me down the hall, past a sleek kitchen with dark stone counters and a sunken living room outfitted in soft leather and warm wood accents. It smells faintly of coffee and cedar. Cozy in a way I wouldn't expect from a place this ostentatious.

We turn a corner, and he stops in front of a door with a brass handle. "This one's yours."

He pushes it open and steps back so I can walk through first.

I pause in the doorway and zero in on the line of windows stretching across the far wall. They're beautiful, floor-to-ceiling, polished clean, with an incredible view, but they're also exposed, too open, too vulnerable. Anyone could see in and -

Stop it. You're on the tenth floor, and the building is crazy secure. You're fine.

I force a breath past my lips and drag my gaze away. The room is beautiful. Muted earth tones. An enormous bed with soft-looking sheets. A small reading nook with a window bench. Bookshelves already half-filled with titles I love. A compact little bathroom off to the side with fluffy white towels stacked neatly on the shelf. A closet I could probably live inside. Everything about it feels intentional, lived in, but not by someone else. It feels made for me.

"Stevie gave us a list," Dallas says from behind me. "Books. Bath products. Candle scents you like. I don't know how she remembered all of it, but she did."

"She always remembers," I murmur, the words tasting like a mix of comfort and guilt as I step inside.

Ollie's nails click softly on the floor as he trots in after me. He circles the room once, sniffs a corner, then hops straight onto the bed like he's claiming it for himself.

Dallas groans. "Seriously, man? Your fluff is going to get everywhere."

Ollie flops down, tongue out, looking entirely unbothered.

I laugh, really laugh, for the first time in what feels like forever. Dallas looks at me, and something in his expression shifts, like the sound of my laughter eased something in him too.

"You can kick him out if you want," he says. "He'll listen. *Sometimes.*"

I shake my head. "No. He's welcome."

He quirks a brow. "He snores."

"I don't mind."

Dallas leans a shoulder against the doorway, watching as I toe off my shoes and sit gingerly on the edge of the bed. Ollie immediately rests his head on my thigh.

"This is… a lot," I say quietly.

Dallas tilts his head. "Too much?"

I look around again. At the care in every detail and the effort they didn't have to make.

"Kind of," I whisper. "It's just… no one's ever done something like this for me before."

Before he can respond, the elevator dings and voices sound from somewhere down the hall.

"I told you she likes strawberry Pocky, not chocolate."

"That was one time. She ate the entire box of the chocolate one."

"That was because there were no other snacks in the safe house, Rome."

I blink.

Dallas gives a small grin. "Sounds like the grocery run was successful."

A second later, Niko and Rome appear in the doorway, each carrying armfuls of bags. Trader Joe's, Whole Foods, even a few from a specialty bakery I love downtown.

They didn't just grab essentials. They got *my* essentials. The snacks I like. The drinks I always stock up on. The stuff you only remember if you've actually been paying attention.

They're still arguing as they walk in, bickering about my dietary preferences, when they catch sight of me sitting on the bed and freeze.

Rome blinks. Niko actually pauses mid-step like he forgot how walking works.

"Didn't think you'd be back so soon." Rome says, clearing his throat. He fishes a box out of one of the bags and tosses it onto the bed. "It's that Mochi ice cream stuff you love so much. Keep it in the back of the freezer so Dallas doesn't steal it."

Dallas' jaw drops. "I don't even like mochi."

"Doesn't stop you from stealing shit."

Niko sets his bags on the dresser and meets my gaze like he's checking for any fractures he might've missed earlier.

"I'm good," I say before he can ask.

He nods then turns and walks away.

Rome ruffles Ollie's head before heading after him, muttering something under his breath about Niko buying off-brand toothpaste.

When it's just the two of us again, Dallas lingers in the doorway. "You want anything else in here?" he asks. "TV? Mini fridge? Sound machine?"

"I think I'm good."

He nods slowly. "Alright. I'll be down the hall if you need anything."

I wait until he's almost gone before I say, "Hey, Dallas?"

He stops and looks over his shoulder.

"Thanks," I say. "For all of this."

His smile is quiet, easy, but his eyes flicker like he's feeling more than he's saying. "Anytime, V."

He walks away, and I sit there with Ollie curled up beside me, his head heavy on my leg, the smell of lemon tea and old book pages in the air.

For the first time in a long time, I don't feel like I'm crashing on someone's couch. I feel like I might belong. And that freaking terrifies me.

NINE

VIOLET

THIS ROOM WAS TAILORED FOR ME. *I KNOW THAT.* I CAN SEE IT IN every detail. The pale gray walls with lavender undertones. The floating bookshelves, already lined with the titles I reread when the world gets too loud. The throw blanket draped across the foot of the bed that I once told Stevie I wanted because it reminded me of the night sky.

Everything about this place is thoughtful. Purposeful. But knowing something was made for you isn't the same as believing you deserve it, and every beautiful detail only serves to remind me that I don't belong here.

Not in this apartment. Not in this quiet. Not in this life that feels like someone else's.

Niko said he killed my attacker. He said it was his bullet that ended his life. But we both know the man was already dead when he got there. Still, he looked me in the eye and gave me a version of the truth I could live with. And I let him. Because I didn't have the strength to argue, and I didn't have it in me to carry the weight of one more thing.

I let him clean up my mess. I let him lie for me. And now

I'm here, wrapped in warmth I didn't earn, in a room I don't deserve, wondering if this is all I'll ever be. A liability. A burden. Something people constantly feel sorry for because it's too broken to function.

I haven't unpacked yet. I just shoved my duffel in the corner and spent the last two hours rearranging the books on the shelves over and over again. First alphabetically, then by height, then by color.

I glance at the closed door. I haven't left my wing since Dallas gave me the tour last night, so I haven't seen any of them today, but I can hear them.

Rome's footsteps are always easy to recognize. They're measured and no-nonsense, like he has somewhere to be. Dallas usually hums when he's walking around. He's almost always off-key, but it never seems to bother him. Niko usually walks around when it's late. I know it's him because he barely makes a sound when he moves, and it's like I can sense his presence more than anything.

They're out there, and I'm in here, and honestly, that distance is the only thing keeping me sane right now.

———

THE NEXT MORNING, I wake up before the sun rises. The apartment is quiet. No creaking floorboards, no low hum of conversation, just stillness.

I tiptoe into the kitchen, careful not to make a sound. It almost feels selfish to be the only one awake in a place this big. I get to reap all the benefits of the space without having to share it with the people that actually pay for it.

I make a single piece of toast, butter it lightly, and pour half a glass of orange juice. Not a drop more. If I keep the dent in supplies small enough, maybe they won't notice. I sit at the far end of the kitchen island with my back to the door, legs pulled up beneath me, and take slow, quiet bites. Then I hear the soft shuffle of claws on hardwood.

Ollie trots out of one of the other wings, tail wagging like he already knew I'd be here. He doesn't bark or whine, thank god, and he's perfectly content with flopping down dramatically at my feet.

"Hey, Ollie," I whisper, nudging his paw with my socked foot. "Was your sleep crappy too?"

He stares up at and blinks. Then yawns like this whole interaction is beneath him.

"Can I tell you a secret?" I ask, leaning down to scratch behind his ears. "You're the easiest one to talk to in this place."

He lets out sigh and looks up at me.

Yep.

He totally agrees.

———

THAT NIGHT, I don't come out for dinner. But I hear them from my room. Low voices, the clatter of dishes, and bursts of laughter that echo down the hall. Someone says something sarcastic. The others groan. I think it's Rome. He always sounds like he's trying not to enjoy himself.

I stare at the pile of protein bars I stuffed into the bottom of my duffel and choose one without checking the flavor. I eat it out of the wrapper, one bite at a time, while scrolling through my phone just to keep my hands busy.

They laugh again, and I tell myself I'm not missing anything.

———

ON DAY THREE, I open my door and find a full plate of breakfast sitting on the floor. Waffles, turkey bacon, and a coffee with extra cream, just how I like it. All still warm. There's no note and I'm fairly certain no one knocked. Still, it's there, waiting for me.

I don't grab it right away. I wait until I'm sure no one's nearby, then I quietly pull the plate inside and sit on the carpet, legs crossed, eating quietly by the door.

Somehow, the gesture is more comforting than anything they could've said aloud.

———

THAT NIGHT, I crack my door open a few inches. Just to listen. Rome and Niko are in the living room, barking at the TV.

I peek out just far enough to see them on the couch with Ollie and PS5 controllers in hand. Dallas walks behind them holding a protein shake and muttering something about not yelling in front of the dog. Rome flips him off, and Niko throws a pillow at his head without looking.

They all laugh. It's not loud, or forced, it's easy. I pull the door shut before they can see me.

———

THE NEXT MORNING, I find Ollie camped outside my room. He's laid out with his head facing the hallway like he's been on patrol all night. His ears twitch when I open the door, and he cracks one eye open and lets out a slow sigh when he sees me.

"I didn't ask for a guard dog," I mumble, crouching down next to him.

His tail thumps against the hardwood.

I sit beside him and rest my head back against the wall. The cool surface seeps into my spine. Maybe I didn't ask for any of this. This house. This safety. This weird cocoon of quiet care that I don't know how to fit into. But it's here. And I don't want to run from it anymore.

———

THAT EVENING, I wander into the kitchen when I smell something rich and buttery.

Rome glances up from the stove, but he doesn't comment on me being there. He doesn't acknowledge the fact that I've been hiding for days. He just nods toward the kitchen island.

"You want a plate?"

I nod.

He sets it in front of me, and I thank him as I take a seat.

Niko's already sitting next to me. His legs are stretched out, and he's flipping through a worn paperback with one hand, while nursing a mug of black coffee with his other. He doesn't look up, but I feel him shift slightly, like he knows I'm here but doesn't want to scare me off by acknowledging it.

Dallas appears ten minutes later. He drops a bag of candy on the counter and slides it silently toward me. Watermelon sour strips. *My favorite.* I open the bag, rip off a piece, and slip it into my mouth.

Dallas fights a smile as he takes a seat beside me. No one asks what changed.No one asks why I finally came out. They just let me sit. Quiet. Awkward. But here. And somehow… that's enough.

TEN

ROME

Violet falls asleep on the couch again. She does that a
lot now. Stays up too late watching k-dramas on low volume,
curled up under the same throw blanket with Ollie tucked at
her side.

I was coming out of my room for water. Now I'm stuck,
frozen halfway down the hall, staring like a creep at the
woman passed out in our living room.

She's wearing one of Dallas's hoodies, oversized and
faded, with the sleeves pulled over her hands. One leg's
draped off the couch, and her face is half-buried in a pillow
that she must've brought out from her room. She looks peaceful. Like she's finally letting herself breathe.

Ollie lifts his head from the floor when he notices me, ears
twitching like he's silently judging me for staring.

Don't worry, Bud, I'm judging me, too.

Violet shifts in her sleep, and the blanket draped over her
slips, sliding down to expose the pair of light blue sleep
shorts she's wearing that do nothing to help the situation. I

exhale through my nose, telling myself not to be weird about it. Just pull the blanket back up and walk away.

Easy.

Gathering my nerves, I inch closer and reach over the back of the couch, straining to grab the corner of the blanket without waking her. It's too far. *Of course it is.*

I circle around, stepping carefully to sit on the edge of the couch beside her and lean over to reach for it again. That's when she moves and rolls straight into me.

The weight of her body presses me back and her cheek lands against my chest with a soft thud. Her arm drapes across my stomach like it's done this a hundred times before. Like I'm hers to hold on to, like I always have been. I freeze and look down at her.

Her face is right there. Her eyes are shut, her lips are parted, and the top of her forehead is pressed against the edge of my shirt collar.

My pulse spikes, and I can already feel the anxiety creeping up.

Don't move, asshole. Don't breathe. Don't ruin this.

I glance at Ollie, desperate for a lifeline.

He's watching from his spot next to her, head resting on his paws, staring up at me like he's annoyed she's snuggling up to me of all people.

I swallow hard, trying not to make a sound.

Her hand shifts slightly, fingers brushing the bottom hem of my t-shirt. She nuzzles in, just the tiniest bit, like even in sleep, she's trying to get closer.

I should get up, I should move, but I don't. I sit there, spine straight, muscles locked, like some kind of coward afraid of his own heartbeat.

She mumbles something against my chest.

"Rome."

It's barely audible, but I hear it. And my jaw tightens

immediately. *She said my fucking name.* I know I shouldn't read into it, but I do.

I stare straight ahead, eyes locked on the far wall like it's gonna give me the answers I need. It doesn't. Neither does Ollie. He just yawns and closes his eyes, clearly over this scene.

Traitor.

Her breath is warm against my chest. The weight of her against me shouldn't feel good, but it does. And that's a problem, because I've been here before.

Not this exact couch, not on this exact night, but this feeling? It's familiar. And the last time I let myself lose control around her, she pretended like it never happened.

I told myself it didn't matter, *but it did*, it still does.

I look down at her again and let my eyes trace the curve of her lashes, the softness of her mouth, and the way she relaxes into me like I'm safe, like I matter. It's a lie. Not from her. She's not even awake, but my mind's already making up stories for itself.

I shift just enough to test her weight. She doesn't stir.

Good.

Slowly, I roll her back over as I reach for the blanket again and tug it up over her shoulders. Her brow twitches like she's about to wake.

I freeze and wait. *Nothing.* Then I slide my arm out from beneath her, moving inch by inch like I'm disarming a bomb.

The second I'm free, I stand up and back away. She curls into the spot I left behind and tucks her hands beneath her cheek like nothing happened, like she didn't just undo me in thirty seconds flat without even opening her eyes.

I glance down at her one last time and take in the faint crease between her brows and the whisper of a frown that never fully leaves.

Then I turn and walk away. Because if I stay, I'll start to

believe this means something. And I've already made that mistake before.

ELEVEN

VIOLET

The scallions hiss as they hit the pan and the scent of garlic permeates through the air. I toss the noodles again and am just about to reach for the sesame oil when my phone buzzes on the counter beside me.

It's a video call from Stevie. She's been doing that a lot lately, now that she has her voice back. I guess the weeks of forced silence turned her into a yapper.

Killing the burner; I wipe my hands on a towel, prop my phone against the paper towel holder, and answer the call. Stevie's face fills my screen, glowing with that soft, hospital-grade lighting.

"Hey," I say, smiling into the camera. "You look better."

"I look like a stitched-up scarecrow," she says dryly.

"Yeah. But, like, a hot one."

Her lips twitch, and she leans back against her pillows with a sigh. Her throat bandages are freshly changed. I can see them peeking out from beneath the edge of her hoodie=.

Around me, the apartment is quiet. Rome and Niko are

still out, and Dallas just left to take Ollie out for a walk before dinner. I shift my camera toward the stove. "Look, I'm making stir-fry."

Stevie squints and cocks her head. "You're cooking for them?"

I pick up the suspicion in her tone immediately.

"It's therapeutic," I say, tossing the wok one more time. "I get to control everything. The temperature. The flavor. How much garlic goes in."

She smiles. "You always go overboard with the garlic."

I roll my eyes. "I'll take that as a compliment."

She watches me for a moment, expression unreadable. "You're… doing okay?"

I nod. "Yup, never been better."

It's not a lie. I am feeling better than I have in a while, but after everything I've endured, I don't know if I'll ever be fully okay.

Before she can press any further, the elevator doors open. I glance up to see Rome stride in, loose hoodie slung over his frame, a drink carrier in one hand and a bakery bag in the other.

Without a word, he sets the milk tea down in front of me.

Strawberry jasmine.

"My favorite." I say, smiling up at him. "How'd you know?"

Rome shrugs. "You only order it every time."

"I'm not that predictable."

He arches a brow. "You're a creature of annoying habits."

I swat at him. "Rude."

He catches my hand midair, smirking. "Honest. And you love it."

"I tolerate it."

Rome notices my phone and his smirk falters. "Is that Stevie?"

I grin and tilt the camera towards him. "Say hi."

Stevie's eyes narrow into tiny slits. "Rome."

He gives her a single chin lift. "Hey, Stevie."

Stevie presses her eyes closed like she's trying to unsee something. "You bought my sister milk tea?"

He nods. "She's nicer when she has sugar."

"Uh-huh."

There's a pause, not a long one, but enough for me to feel the tension between them.

Rome turns back to me. "I'll let you two catch up."

"Thanks." I say, reaching up to kiss his cheek.

It's quick, light, more instinct than anything else, but it still stuns him. I feel his body go rigid. His gaze catches mine for a heartbeat, before he clears his throat and steps back like I just brandished a weapon. He opens his mouth to say something, then closes it again.

"I, uh…" He gestures over his shoulder. "Forgot to put the other stuff in the fridge."

"Rome," I say, eyeing him warily, "Is everything good?"

I expect him to laugh. Or shrug. Or do anything, really. But he just backs away like I burned him.

"It's fine," he says, and disappears down the hall.

I glance at my screen. Stevie hasn't moved. She's staring at me with her head tilted and her brow furrowed, like she's trying to solve a complex math problem in her head.

"You kissed him," she says.

"On the cheek. It was a thank-you kiss."

Though I can't remember the last time I could get that close to someone without flinching.

"Sure." She sits up straighter in her hospital bed, the movement stiff but precise. "That's what it looked like."

I stay quiet.

She doesn't.

"Please be careful."

"I am," I say, even though I'm not sure it's true.

Stevie sighs and worries her lip. "Look, I know you're grateful they were there when you needed them. I get it. But you're still healing, Alex. You're vulnerable. And they -"

I flinch.

Alex. That name doesn't belong to me anymore. It hasn't for a while now, but I still let her use it. She already lost the old me. I didn't have the heart to make her to lose anything else.

"They're my friends." I say a little sharper than I mean to. "They've been nothing but good to me."

"I know. But that's not the point."

"Then what is?"

Stevie's eyes flick to something off-screen. She takes a second too long to respond, and when she does, her voice is much softer.

"You shouldn't blur the lines, Al. You're there because you need a safe place to stay, not... anything else. I know that sounds hypocritical coming from me, but I'm only saying this because I don't want you to get hurt."

I go quiet, because I don't know what to say. Whatever's happening between me and Rome, me and all of them really, isn't defined. It's not clear, and maybe she's right. Maybe blurring the lines is a bad idea.But also... *what if it isn't?*

"I just think," Stevie adds carefully, "you should be careful. At least until you're back home and your head's clear."

"Why?" I ask, voice smaller than I mean it to be.

Her face softens. "Because you've already been hurt enough. You don't need more heartbreak on top of everything else."

I nod slowly. Not because I fully agree with her, but because I don't know what else to do.

"I've got to go," she says. "My nurse is here. Promise me you'll keep things simple with them. Just for now?"

I hesitate. "Okay."

She nods and ends the call. The screen goes dark, and I sit in silence for a moment, listening to the faint tap of rain against the windows.

Rome's milk tea is still sitting untouched beside me. I pick it up, take one sip, and quietly wonder if she's right.

TWELVE

VIOLET

It's been a few days since my call with Stevie, and I haven't seen much of Rome since. I'd be lying if I said I didn't miss having his grouchy self around, but I think it's for the best, for now at least.

Some time apart will do us both some good. In the last few weeks, I've gotten way too comfortable around him, and the last thing I want is to make him feel uneasy in his own home.

The apartment is quiet tonight, but it's not empty. Not really. Rome's mug is still by the sink. The one Dallas gave him as a joke that says *World's Okayest Boss*. Niko's boots, the laced-up leather ones he always leaves by the elevator, are still right where he kicked them off. Dallas's hoodie is still flung over the back of the couch with the sleeves rumpled like he peeled it off mid-stride. And then there's Ollie, curled up at my feet, tracking me with his big brown eyes as I move around the kitchen.

For the first time in weeks, I'm the only one home. But in a weird way, I'm not alone.

The stove hisses softly behind me. I stir the sauce, then

lean over to check the pasta. Everything smells warm and delicious, like spices and garlic and home.

I'm not used to this feeling, the safety, the *peace*. It still feels like I haven't earned it, like any second, someone's going to come in and take it all away.

I glance down to see Ollie watching me with those big, hopeful brown eyes. His ears are perked and his tail is wagging, like I'm putting on the most exciting show of his life.

It's not like I'm doing anything impressive. He probably can smell the chicken I'm pan-frying and is just waiting for the moment I break and sneak him a little taste.

"Not happening, Prince Ali," I murmur, even though my resistance is already slipping. "Your Papa will kill me."

His tail thumps once on the hardwood, like he's trying to argue and I shake my head. The only thing bigger than his stomach is his attitude.

I grab a handful of basil and start dicing, slowly and steadily. Over the last few weeks, cooking dinner for the guys has become a kind of ritual for me. It's the one thing I can do to say *thank you* without having to actually say it.

My phone buzzes on the counter. I glance at it, fingers still slick with olive oil.

Unknown Number.

1 New Message.

I wipe my hand on a dishtowel and open the text.

I miss you.

My fingers hesitate over the screen and my chest squeezes. Not all at once, slowly, like there's something coiling around my ribs.

I swallow hard and set the phone back down. *It's probably just the wrong number.* I shake my head, pick up the knife, and start dicing again.

Another buzz. Another notification.

> You were so pretty when you cried, my perfect girl.

Perfect girl.

There was only one man that ever called me that. It's the same man who bought me. Who caged me. Who broke me, over and over again, just because he could. *This has to be some kind of sick joke.*

The knife slips.

"Shit -"

Pain lances through my thumb. The blade clatters to the floor, and blood spills fast.

I stagger back from the counter, grabbing the closest towel. My breath punches out in short, shallow gasps. Ollie whines, scrambling to his feet. He presses his head against my leg and licks my ankle like he knows something's wrong.

I crouch and grip the towel tighter. "I'm fine," I whisper.

But I'm not. I can't breathe.

My knees buckle, and I grip the edge of the counter to stay upright. *God*, I need to calm down. Just because he has my number doesn't mean he knows where I am. He could've gotten it anywhere. A database. A leak. He's in my phone, but that doesn't mean he's here.

This place is hidden. The locks are reinforced. The windows are tinted. I'm safe. *Aren't I?*

I close my eyes, trying to steady myself, trying to believe the lie. The elevator dings and I snap my head up, heart stuttering in my chest.

"V?"

Dallas' voice hits me like a floodlight in a dark cave. I don't answer him. *I can't.* I'm barely holding it together as it is.

He rounds the corner and freezes mid-step. His eyes flick from my face to the towel wrapped around my hand, then to the floor where the knife lies in a puddle of blood, and something sharp flickers across his face.

"Shit, V."

In three long strides, he's kneeling in front of me, his voice lower now but no less urgent. "What happened? Did you fall? Did someone-?"

"No," I whisper. "I just… wasn't paying attention and cut myself. It's nothing."

He doesn't look convinced. His gaze flicks over me again, scanning for other injuries like he's expecting more damage. His jaw clenches as he reaches for the first aid kit under the sink.

I try to speak again, to brush it off, but my throat locks up.

Dallas is so close. Close enough, I can smell his cologne and the faint scent of mint on his breath. He focuses, hands gentle but firm as he unwraps the towel, careful not to jostle me more than he has to.

"You're shaking," he says quietly. "Are you cold?"

I shake my head. "No. I'm fine."

I'm not, and we both know it.

Dallas doesn't press me on it, he just keeps working. His brow furrows in concentration as he cleans the cut and wraps it in gauze. He moves like he's done this a hundred times, but the tension in his shoulders tells me this time's different.

Ollie presses closer, head now resting across my feet. I sit there and try not to fall apart.

Say it. Tell him what happened. Tell him someone texted you. That you think it's *him.* That he's torturing you all over again.

I open my mouth. Dallas looks up to meet my eyes, and I see it. The softness. The hope. The quiet, unspoken question he's too afraid to ask.

Why can't you trust me?

And I break inside a little more, because I *want* to trust him. I want to fall into him, to tell him I'm scared and that I don't know what to do. But I'm already holding on by a thread, and if I let go, if I let him see the truth, I'll unravel. And he'll see the mess and finally decide he wants no part in it.

So I force a smile, even as it trembles on the edges. "Thanks for patching me up," I say softly.

Dallas holds my gaze. His expression doesn't change, but something in his eyes dims. Just a little, like he knows I'm holding something back. But he doesn't push the subject. He just nods. "Anytime, V."

The moment he leaves, I reach for my phone again. The messages are still there. My thumb hovers over the thread, and for one breath, I consider running after him and showing it to him. Telling him everything and letting him carry some of the weight, but the thought sours fast. I know exactly what will happen if I do.

He'll look at me the same way people always do when they realize I'm broken beyond repair, and he'll realize I'm not worth the trouble. I've already been the fragile girl they had to rescue once. I can't be her again. *Not now.* Not when I'm finally building a life here.

My chest still feels tight, but my hands stay steady as I swipe left and hit delete. The messages vanish.I tuck my phone back into my pocket and force my shoulders to straighten.

If ignoring it makes me a coward, so be it. Better a coward than a burden.

THIRTEEN

NIKO

I<small>T'S TWO A.M. AND</small> I'<small>M RESTLESS AGAIN.</small> I'<small>M</small> *ALWAYS* <small>RESTLESS.</small> Sleep never comes easily to me. Not when it's dark, not when it's quiet. That's when the noise in my head is at full volume.

So I move from room to room. Wall to wall. Until I eventually end up here, standing shirtless in the kitchen.

The kitchen is empty. The lights are off, and the fridge is quietly humming. I open it even though I'm not hungry. Eating is just something to do to pass the time.

Rows of meal-prepped containers stare back at me, filled with grilled chicken breast, sweet potatoes, and broccoli. All of them labeled in careful handwriting. *Violet's handwriting.* They must be for Rome.

I slide the containers aside and dig deep into the back of the fridge and find an old prepackaged snack kit with crackers, cheese and turkey in it. I peel back the plastic, stack the meat and cheese on a cracker, and take a bite

"That's nostalgic." A voice calls out from somewhere in the darkness.

It's Vi.

I don't jump. I never do, but her sudden appearance does catch me off guard. She's barefoot in a sleep shirt that hits mid-thigh, with sleeves too long for her arms. Her long lavender hair's a mess, and her eyes are tired. She looks like she was pulled out of sleep mid-dream, or mid-nightmare.

"You want one?" I ask, holding up another stack.

She gives me a look. "You're literally eating sadness."

I shrug and chew. "Gets the job done."

She crosses the kitchen and opens the pantry, already scanning for something better. "Let me make you something."

I stop chewing. "You don't have to."

"I want to."

I shake my head. "It's late. I don't want you going out of your way."

"Oh." Her voice drops just a little. "Right. I forgot you don't really like my cooking."

Fuck.

"That's not it," I say quickly. "I just…"

I trail off, then sigh.

She looks confused, maybe even a little hurt. I don't tell her the truth. It's not the food I avoid, it's *her*. She's soft in a way I'm not built for and eventually, I'll break her.

"I just don't want you to waste your time." The words slip out too soft, too honest.

She frowns. "I wouldn't be wasting my time."

"Thank you, but really, I'm okay."

Violet nods as she chews on her lower lip and leans against the counter. She picks at the edge of her sleeve, looking like she regrets walking in here.

I should've just let her make me something. *I'm such a fucking asshole.*

I go to toss the packaging, and when I glance back, her eyes aren't on my face anymore, they're on my chest.

My muscles instinctively tighten under her gaze. Fuckers are enjoying having her eyes on them. She stares at the ink that crawls over my chest and ribs and spills down onto my arms. A tiger, sharp and angry. A camellia bloom carved in red. And a demon wrapped in smoke.

"Your tattoos," she says softly, "they're beautiful."

"Thanks. Painful too."

For a second, I imagine her with ink of her own. Something sexy and artistic, hidden in a place that no one else can see. And *fuck,* I shouldn't be picturing that.

She tugs at her sleeve again. "They look like it."

Her gaze is slow, curious, and it lingers a little too long. She clenches her hands, like her fingers want to touch the ink, but she doesn't trust her control over them.

"You ever think about getting one?"

"A tattoo?"

I nod.

She hesitates. "I never wanted one." She says a little wistfully.

"Why not?"

Her shoulders lift in a small shrug.

"Fear of needles?" I offer.

Her brow furrows. "Something like that."

I nod, but I'm watching her now and I notice the way her shoulders tense and her eyes flick away. She's *lying.* I'm just not sure about what.

Vi doesn't speak again. She just stands there, quiet in the kitchen's silence, with her gaze fixed on something that isn't there. I catch the shift. The way her shoulders sink, the way her eyes dull and her fingers still, like her mind's slipped somewhere she doesn't want to be. Somewhere heavy. Somewhere haunting.

I know that feeling, and now I understand why she offered to cook for me in the middle of the night. It's that need to do something, anything, to push off the weight pressing down on you. To distract yourself. To feel useful. Even if it's only temporary.

"You know what." I say, getting her attention. "I'm still a little hungry. Mind throwing together a grilled cheese for me?"

Her face lifts, just slightly, and she nods her head.

She moves quickly, like she's afraid I'll change my mind if she isn't fast enough.

I sit at the island while she works, watching her.

She knows exactly what she's doing. She's calm, focused, and moves like the kitchen is hers, and always has been. Butter hits the pan and sizzles on contact. The rich scent perfumes in the air instantly.

While she's distracted, I let myself take a long look at her.

She's pretty even when she isn't trying to be.

Violet 's beauty is haunting. Ethereal and out of place in the best possible way. Her lavender hair cascades down her back like silk, and her emerald eyes are shadowed with things she never says out loud. There's a sadness to her that makes her seem older than she is.

She moves through the world carefully, as if she's trying not to take up too much space, or get in anyone's way. As if she's been told her whole life to shrink, and even now, even here, she forgets she doesn't have to.

Her fingers brush mine when she passes me the plate, *barely,* but it's enough to remind me just how dangerous this is.

"I'm going to head back to bed." She says, offering me a soft smile, as she heads out of the kitchen. "Thanks for keeping me company."

"Thank you for the food."

As soon as I hear her door click shut, I take a bite of the sandwich, and it's good. No, fuck that, it's the best grilled cheese I've ever had. And that's a problem, because now I'll want more. And the last thing a man like me should ever do is want. Especially when it's something he knows he shouldn't have.

FOURTEEN

VIOLET

The rain hasn't stopped all morning. It drips in slow, steady lines down the floor-to-ceiling windows, blurring the skyline until the buildings look like ghosts. I've been staring at the same drop for ten minutes, watching it race the others before it finally disappears into the sill.

My phone sits beside me on the windowsill, lighting up every few minutes. Another incoming text. Another message I won't be reading. *He's* been messaging me nonstop lately. I delete them as soon as they come in, but they still leave a lingering effect on me.

It's not fear exactly. *Not anymore.* Now it's morphed into this strange pressure. Like I'm standing on a frozen lake, and every vibration of my phone deepens the cracks in the ice. I try to ignore it, but deep down I know it's only a matter of time before it inevitably rips the floor right out from underneath me.

It's been a couple of weeks since the night in the kitchen with Niko, and I've spent most of that time pretending it didn't happen. I tell myself it was nothing, just a late-night snack, but maybe that's because the truth feels too raw.

Niko pulled me out of my head that night. Not with some grand gesture, not by forcing me to talk, but with the smallest distraction. Like he knew exactly how to reach me without making it worse. It wasn't the first time, either. After the attack, when I could barely move or speak, he broke through the fog with ease. He didn't push. He didn't hover. He just... knew. The right words. The right silences. The exact thread to pull to bring me back to myself.

That's why I've been avoiding him. Niko understands the dark places in my head in a way no one else does. When he looks at me, it's like he can see all of it - the cracks, the shadows, the ugly parts I don't let anyone touch.

And I *hate* how exposed that makes me feel.

My phone buzzes again. I flinch and glance down at the screen. It's a video call. From Stevie. I hesitate just long enough for the guilt to set in, then I swipe to answer.

Her face fills the screen, looking better than it has in weeks. Her hair's clean and tied back. She's sitting up in bed with a mug of tea in one hand and a blanket draped over her shoulders.

"You look like shit," she says playfully.

"Thanks," I mutter. "You're glowing."

She smirks. "The fluorescents are very forgiving."

I smile, then glance down at my fingernails before continuing. "Any news on the attacker?"

Stevie's expression shifts. "Yeah. A little. We know he was hired through an agency. One of those black-market fixers who deals in contracted muscle. They didn't give him a name or a photo of a target. Just instructed him to grab the girl and gave him cash and coordinates."

My stomach tightens. "And?"

"That's where the paper trail ends. Tristan said the payment logs were scrubbed. No client listed. Whoever hired him covered their tracks well. We're still digging, but it's slow."

I nod, trying not to let the frustration show on my face.

"Don't worry, though," she adds quickly. "Nothing else weird has happened in weeks. And now that we know someone's after us, everyone has got their guard up."

She says it like that should be enough, like the problem's been cornered and locked away. But it hasn't. Not when my phone won't stop buzzing with new messages. Not when I'm still deleting his words before I have the nerve to read them all the way through.

"You sure you're doing okay?" She asks, her voice quiet but direct. "You look like there's something on your mind."

My pulse kicks up.

"I'm good," I say quickly. "Just going a little stir-crazy."

"Same." She breathes.

A long silence stretches between us.

"I should be cleared to leave the hospital at the end of next week," she says eventually. "Ez is already planning to carry me out bridal-style."

I manage a half-smile. "I wouldn't expect anything less."

Her eyes soften. "You know you could come home with me too, if you want? The guys amped up the security so it'll be super secure."

I smile and shake my head. "I'm good here, but thank you."

Stevie nods, then pauses for a beat.

"How are things with the guys?" She asks casually, too casually.

"They're fine."

"Fine?" She presses.

I keep my tone neutral. "They're nice. They're respectful. Things are good."

"That's good."

She says it like she really means it, then adds, "Still. It

must be hard living with three attractive guys. I imagine it feels…" She pauses. "…complicated?"

And there it is.

I straighten slightly. "It's not like that."

"I didn't say it was."

"Yeah, but you're implying it."

"Okay, yes. But I just want to make sure you're not getting too attached to living with them."

I bristle.

"I'm not."

Stevie raises an eyebrow. "You sure? Because the last time I heard you this defensive, you were twelve and trying to convince me you didn't like your math tutor."

"I *didn't* like him."

"You cried when he quit the after-school program."

I scowl. "I was a kid back then. This isn't the same thing."

"Then what is it?"

"I don't know," I snap, voice cracking. "Okay? I don't know what this is. I don't know what they feel, or if I'm just some broken thing they're trying to fix. But for once, I feel wanted. I feel safe. Isn't that enough?"

Stevie goes quiet.

Then softly, she says: "I get it. I really do. With how we grew up, safety was rare. But sometimes it's hard to tell the difference between kindness and something more. I just want to make sure you aren't misconstruing things."

That stings.

"You think I'm reading it wrong?"

"No," she says gently. "I think you're vulnerable. They're all attractive, and they're taking care of you. That's a dangerous mix."

My throat tightens.

"You really think I'm that pathetic?"

"Alex."

"You think I'm so unlovable that the idea of them wanting me is a fantasy?"

"That's not what I said."

"Yeah, but it's what you meant."

I can feel the heat building behind my eyes.

"I'm not confused," I whisper. "And I don't need you reminding me I'm hard to love. I already figured that out on my own."

Stevie's expression cracks.

"Al... I didn't mean it like that. If anything, you're too lovable. I just- I just want you to be careful."

I end the call before she can say anything else.

The screen goes black. My reflection stares back, eyes red-rimmed and raw.

What if she's right? What if this thing I'm feeling isn't real? What if I let myself believe they care, only to find out later I was wrong?

I blink hard, forcing the tears to stand down. I will not cry, not over this, but I can still feel the sting of her words. *"Sometimes it's hard to tell the difference between kindness and something more."*

Yeah. Tell me about it.

FIFTEEN

ROME

VIOLET IS FADING AGAIN. NOT DRAMATICALLY. THERE'S NO slammed doors or screaming matches. It's happening slowly, and it feels like she's trying to make herself disappear without any of us noticing. But *I* notice, and I can't fucking stand to see it.

I tell myself to ignore it, that it isn't my problem or my place to care. She's been through hell, and I'm not entitled to her attention or her warmth. But I *do* care, and I feel everything. The shift, the silence, the absence.

She used to love working in the kitchen. She'd be in there cooking every night and every morning, like clockwork. Always trying new recipes. Sometimes with ingredients I've never even heard of, and always begging us to taste-test her creations.

She even got Niko, the man who treats enjoyment like it's a personal threat, to come to the table. The food was always good, but it wasn't about that. It was the way she'd watch us nervously as we took our first bite and the way her eyes would light up when she'd see our reactions.

That was the part that got me. The excitement, the spark, like, for just a second, she stopped worrying about everything else going on and could just be happy. No fear of an imminent threat. No drowning in all the shit in her head. Just pure, unadulterated joy.

And now?

The kitchen's been quiet for days. No sizzling pans. No k-pop music blasting. No Violet. And it's not just me she's hiding from. She barely talks to Dallas and Niko. And poor Ollie has been camped outside her bedroom nearly every night.

She's not just shutting me out. She's shutting all of us out. She skips meals. Spends most of the day in her room with the door closed. She only comes out to eat, and even then, she never lingers in our shared spaces. She doesn't tease us. Doesn't ask questions. She just disappears. And I hate that it irks me.

I try to tell myself it's for logistical reasons. That it's easier to monitor her when she's visible and easier to keep her safe when she's predictable. But deep down, I know that's bullshit. I *miss* her.

Not the version of her we rescued, the one who flinched when we came near her. I miss the girl who started fighting her way back. The one who asked Niko if he poisoned her cereal with that ridiculous deadpan expression. The one who laughed under her breath when Dallas tripped over Ollie and tried to play it cool. The one who kissed my cheek like it meant nothing and ruined me for the rest of the week. I miss *that* Violet, and I don't know how the hell we lost her.

It's been three days. Three days of icy silence and half-glances. Three days of her shrinking away every time we step into a room. Three days of trying not to care. Of failing.

And today? Today I snap.

She's on the balcony when I find her. With her head down, headphones on, and her face deep in one of her books.

I step out to join her. She doesn't look up, doesn't acknowledge me at all. Just keeps staring at the words on the page like they're the most interesting fucking thing in the world.

I grind my jaw and speak.

"Get up. You're coming with me."

That gets her attention.

She stops reading, but she still keeps her head down. "Where?"

"Out."

"We're not supposed to leave."

"I'm aware."

She finally looks up. Her expression is unreadable.

"Then why are you -"

"I'm not asking."

I jerk my head toward the front door. "Let's go."

"Rome -"

"Move."

It comes out too sharp, but I don't take it back.

She stares at me like I've grown another head. She's probably waiting for me to backpedal and tell her this is all some kind of joke.

"I don't want to go anywhere with you," she says.

"Good thing you don't have a choice. You've got ten seconds before I throw you over my shoulder."

"You're insane."

"Probably."

She crosses her arms, still not moving. "You're not my boss."

"No, but I am the one driving. So unless you want to be dragged to the car barefoot, I suggest you grab some fucking shoes."

She lets out a sharp breath. "Fine. But if I end up dead in a ditch somewhere, I'm coming back to haunt your ass."

Then she storms off to grab her sneakers from the coat closet.

Five minutes later, she's in my passenger seat. Legs crossed, arms folded, and her hoodie zipped to her chin. She doesn't look at me as I start the car. She doesn't speak to me at all. But she came, and she hasn't cursed me out yet. So, I'll consider that progress. For now.

SIXTEEN

VIOLET

I DON'T ASK WHERE WE'RE GOING, AND AS ROME DRIVES through the city, he doesn't offer.

The silence in the car is thick and we're both waiting to see who breaks first.

It *won't* be me.

As we wind our way deeper into the city, I keep my arms crossed and my eyes locked on everything else but him. The buildings get taller, the streets get tighter, and somewhere along the way, the air changes and becomes brighter, louder, busier.

Rome turns the corner and pulls up behind a barricade where foot traffic takes over.

I realize where we are, and for a second, my brain short-circuits.

Red lanterns hang in rows overhead, hundreds of them, casting a soft, golden glow over the street. They move slightly with the breeze, bobbing like fireflies strung up on wire. Beneath them, the entire block is alive.

Booths line both sides of the street under white canopies,

packed with vendors shouting in a mix of English, Cantonese, and Mandarin. The scent of grilled meat and roasted garlic hits me first. Then comes the sweetness of candied ginger, fried dough, syrupy milk tea.

There are signs in the windows of buildings that tower around us, hand-painted banners with brushstroke lettering I can't read. Fire escapes line the sides of old brick buildings, some lit by warm yellow bulbs, others dark. It's beautiful in a way that's not polished or planned. It's layered and lived in and so freaking alive.

Rome finds a spot to park, and climbs out of the car without a word. I scramble to keep up, and as soon as I step out onto the street, the noise swallows me. Laughter, fryers popping, music coming from at least three different sources, and the colors. God, the *colors*. I stand frozen in the middle of it all, overwhelmed but buzzing.

Rome comes up beside me. "You said you always wanted to go to a night market."

I glance over. "You remember that?"

"You talk a lot. Some of it occasionally sticks."

We walk slowly, and Rome stays close with his hands in his pockets and his shoulders tense.

He lets me drag him from stall to stall without complaint. I don't buy anything. I just browse while listening, smelling, and absorbing.

There's a vendor expertly folding dumplings. Another is flipping scallion pancakes on a flat-top grill like he's done it a thousand times. A little girl runs past us, with her mother following close behind, chasing a balloon down the street and laughing when it floats out of reach.

The noise, the lights, the smells, it's overwhelming and somehow exactly what I need. My brain quiets. My skin stops crawling. I'm not waiting for my phone to buzz, or flinching every time someone passes too close.

For the first time in a while, the world isn't suffocating.

Something sizzles behind me, and the scent hits. Sweet soy sauce, toasted sesame oil, and something just starting to burn.

It smells exactly like the stir-fry I made last month. The one that had Niko hovering by the kitchen, waiting for a second plate.

For a second, I can almost feel the cold tile under my feet again. Hear the sizzle of the pan. See the way Rome leaned in to say, *"You're burning the garlic,"* and still ended up cleaning his plate anyway.

I don't know when I stopped doing things that made me feel good. Cooking used to help. It gave me something to control. Something that made other people happy. Maybe that's why I liked it so much.

I liked who I was in the kitchen. Focused. Present. Not afraid to take up space. I want her back.And I think that's why Rome brought me here. Not to cheer me up, not to fix me, but because he knew I needed a place to remember that I'm still capable of feeling good things.

We stop at a dessert stall. The glass case glows with rows of golden egg tarts, their glossy tops slightly cracked from the heat. The smell coming from the stall is unreal. Rich, warm, and buttery.

I hop in the line, unable to resist the temptation.I glance back at Rome and he gives me a quick smile as he studies our surroundings. I fight the urge to laugh at how out of place he looks. Not only is his 6'4' frame practically towering over everyone surrounding us, but his posture is stiff as hell, like he bracing for an ambush at any moment.

It's sweet though, the way he brought me here. He pays a lot more attention to me than I thought he did.

I look back again, searching for him in the crowd, but I can't find him anywhere. Panic blooms in my chest and makes it harder to breathe.

He must've just stepped away. He'll be back. It's fine.

But it's not, because now it feels like everything's closing in on me.

The noise swells, the crowd shifts, and suddenly, paranoia creeps in. I study the crowd, checking every face like I'm expecting to see *my monster* staring back at me.

I don't, but my eyes keep frantically searching for him anyway, like my body refuses to believe it's safe, now that I'm out here all alone.

When I finally spot Rome again, a few booths down, my chest eases a little. Not enough to feel totally safe, but enough to breathe again. *Rome's still here. Still close.*

The vendor helping him is an older woman, with long dark hair pulled into a braid and reading glasses perched on her nose. She says something to Rome, and he smiles at her as he responds. The woman laughs, quiet and knowing, then she points to something on her table.

Rome pays cash for it and tucks something into his jacket before heading back over to me. I wipe the sheen of sweat off my forehead and pretend not to notice.

———

WE FIND a spot to sit under a canopy of string lights strung between two buildings. There's a small fountain nearby, bubbling faintly under the noise. The crowd thins here and the air feels cooler, softer.

Rome sits beside me on the edge of the curb and cocks a brow when he sees the over stuffed box of tarts I bought.

"What?" I say, narrowing my eyes. "They're delicious."

I pull one out and take a bite. The pastry shatters between my teeth. The crust is flaky, still warm, and the custard center is soft and just sweet enough. I nod in approval and keep chewing.

Rome studies me.

"You wanna try one?" I ask, shoving the box towards him.

"I don't eat things that look like they belong in a dollhouse."

I snort. "It's an egg tart."

He shrugs. "Still suspicious."

I take another bite and feel some of the filling smear across my cheek. I plan to wipe it, but Rome gets there first.

He leans in, closer than he has all night, and swipes his thumb across my cheek. His touch is warm, firm, and way too gentle for a man as large as he is. He wipes it off on a napkin and tosses it in the trash without a word. My skin burns where he touched me, and not in a bad way.

For a while, we say nothing. Then, without warning, he reaches into his jacket and sets something beside me. A bracelet. It's black, handwoven, with a small dark stone set in the center.

"Is that for me?"

He shrugs. "It's black tourmaline, figured it'd match the whole gloomy-loner thing you've got going on lately."

I laugh once, softly, and slip it on. It fits perfectly.

"You've been quiet lately," he says. "Different."

I pick at the wrapper of my tart. "I've been thinking."

"About?"

"Just... stuff." I say, averting my gaze.

"Did something happen?"

I shake my head. "Not really. I just talked to my sister."

His jaw flexes. "And?"

"She said some... things."

"What things?"

I fidget with the bracelet on my wrist, trying to delay my answer. "That I'm confused. That you guys are just being nice and I'm misinterpreting your kindness for... something else."

He goes quiet for a long moment. Then says, "Do you think that night meant nothing to me?"

"What?"

"That night when we brought you home from the hospital," he says, his voice lower now. "When you asked me to stay."

My stomach dips and I freeze.

I thought that was Dallas.

My grip tightens on the box in my lap, the cardboard creasing under my fingers. *The warmth, the safety, the way I finally let go.* It was all Rome and I never knew.

He held me when I broke. He *stayed*. He even went out to get me donuts in the morning, and I was a jerk to him. My chest tightens. *I can't believe that was him.*

"That night meant something to me, Violet." He says, his voice is low, steady, like he's releasing a confession that's been weighing on his chest for too long. "Still does."

I meet his eyes, and something in me cracks. I don't think. *I can't.* Not with his words echoing in my chest. Not with the way he's looking at me, like he's waiting to see if I believe him.

I lean in, closing the space between us one breath at a time, and when he doesn't pull back. When he stays perfectly still, letting me come to him. I kiss him.

It's soft at first, hesitant, like I'm testing a boundary neither of us has spoken aloud. His lips are warm, *still,* but not pulling back, not stopping me. My hand drifts to his jaw without thinking. His stubble scrapes the tips of my fingers, rough and real and grounding.

Then he kisses me back, and I stop breathing. It's the kind of kiss that feels like a warning and a promise all wrapped into one. His mouth moves over mine with a quiet hunger, restrained but deep.

His hand wraps around the back of my neck, anchoring me. I feel it in my chest, in my stomach, and in my thighs. Heat blooms low and steady beneath my skin. It's dizzying.

His breath brushes my lips, and when he pulls back, I don't open my eyes right away. My pulse is in my throat. My fingers are still digging into the fabric of his jacket. I feel flushed, breathless, like I just did something reckless I can't take back, but I don't regret it.

When I finally open my eyes, he's watching me. He doesn't look confused, or angry, but he's still unreadable.

I don't speak. Neither does he, but I can still feel the kiss lingering between us, echoing in the silence.

———

As we make our way back to the car, I let myself believe I can have this. That the life I'm building with him, *with all of them*, is safe, whole, and permanent. But then I think about the fact that I've been lying to them, and I can already see the way he'll look at me when the truth comes out. He won't be angry or disappointed. He'll just be done with me. And when that happens, I'll have no one to blame but myself.

SEVENTEEN

VIOLET

It's been a couple of days since I kissed Rome. We haven't talked about it. Haven't acknowledged it, but things have changed between us. It's not a bad change. It's just… different, but in a way that feels good. *I think.*

I don't know. I'm honestly still having a hard time processing my feelings about it and sitting here toying with the bracelet he got me - the one I haven't taken off since he slipped it on - probably isn't helping.

I know it's just a bracelet. That giving it to me probably didn't mean much to him at all. But I'm weirdly attached to it now.

God, if Stevie ever finds out what happened between us that night, I'd never hear the end of it. Especially after she warned me to be careful. That night will just have to stay between Rome and me. At least until I can figure out how I feel about everything.

MY EYES ARE GLUED to the TV as the two leads in my favorite K-Drama move towards each other in slow motion.

"Oh, my God," I gasp.

They move one step closer, then another. The rain is coming down hard, and it's dripping down their faces and soaking their clothes, but their eyes are locked on each other like magnets. They're about to kiss.

I freeze, my mouth full of half-chewed potato chips, my blanket bunched around my knees, and my breath caught in my throat. And then -

DING.

The elevator chimes, and I bolt upright and nearly launch myself off the couch. My bag of chips goes flying. The blanket twists around my ankles, and my heart punches out of my chest.

What the hell?

Heavy, frantic footsteps thunder through the hallway as a voice calls out. "Shit. Shit. Where the hell are my keys?"

I scramble off the couch and run to the hallway to see Dallas tearing through the entryway, hair wild, face pale.

He looks up, eyes locking on me. "Ollie slipped his collar," he says, out of breath. "He saw a bird and just... he ran."

My stomach drops. "He ran?"

"Into traffic." Dallas's voice breaks. "I- I couldn't catch him. I came back to get my car keys. I didn't know what else to do."

"Let's go," I say, already shoving my feet into sneakers. "I'm coming with you."

***

The elevator feels like it's taking forever. Dallas is pacing, muttering under his breath, and rubbing the back of his neck as he tries to hold himself together. I bounce on the balls of my feet, nerves vibrating through my whole body. The thought of Ollie alone in the street, scared and confused, absolutely guts me.

"He's smart," I say, trying to keep my voice steady. "He knows his way around."

"But he's reckless." Dallas counters. "And this city's full of fucking cars."

His voice cracks and that's when I realize, he's not just worrying, he's terrified. If something happens to Ollie, I don't think Dallas will ever be able to forgive himself.

The second the elevator doors open, we're running.

The car peels out of the garage and into the city. Dallas is gripping the wheel so tight his knuckles are white. I've never seen him like this. Stripped of all his usual charm and filled with nothing but raw, frantic energy.

"I'm so fucking stupid." He mutters under his breath.

I glance over. "Don't say that."

He shakes his head, laughing without humor. "Why not? It's true. Everyone knows it."

"I don't," I say quietly.

"I didn't even graduate high school," he mumbles, eyes locked on the road. "Can't be more obvious than that."

I bite my lower lip. "That doesn't mean anything. There are tons of reasons smart people have a hard time in high school."

"Yeah? Like what?"

I swallow. "Like… trying to stay awake in class after cleaning up broken dishes all night. Or praying your dad doesn't overdose while you're at school. Or not having enough food in the house and being too hungry to focus."

He goes still.

"The only reason I graduated is because my sister took the brunt of it. So, I'm sure you had your reasons."

Dallas looks at me and I can tell he wasn't expecting that kind of grace.

He nods slowly, jaw tight. "Yeah. I did."

We hit a red light, and he drops his gaze. "I was seventeen. And she was my English teacher."

The air in the truck goes still.

"She used to stay after school with me. Said I had potential. Said I just needed someone to believe in me."

His voice twists into something sharp. Bitter.

"Then she started touching me. Saying if I didn't give her what she wanted, she'd fail me. Said no one would believe a kid like me. Especially not some dumb country boy."

My fingers dig into my thighs.

"So I stopped showing up. Stopped trying. I dropped out just before I turned eighteen."

He drags a hand through his hair, forcing a laugh that doesn't quite reach his eyes. "Guess I've always thought my only real value was how I looked. The face. The body. The smile."

"Dallas," I whisper.

"It's fine," he says quickly, leveling his eyes on the road again. "Not like it matters now. I figured out how to be useful. Strong. Reliable. The guy people call when they want something handled."

"That's not all you are."

"Yeah, it is."

"No," I push, soft but firm. "You're more than your body. More than what she did to you. You're more than the guy who handles things. You're the guy who cares."

He doesn't respond, but his grip on the wheel loosens, just slightly, and I can tell something uncoiled in him.

We drive a few more blocks in silence. Outside the window, the city blurs by. The world hasn't changed, but something between us has. Dallas reaches for the radio and turns the volume up just enough to hear the bass of the music pumping through the speakers.

It's not a song I recognize, but the soft beat fills the space between us. His fingers tap against the wheel, not from nerves now, but something steadier, and for just a second, I let myself breathe, too.I rest my forehead against the window, letting the sound of the music fill the silence inside me.

The panic over Ollie hasn't passed, but Dallas's story is still echoing in my head. His childhood held a different kind of pain than mine, but it was painful just the same. I want to reach over and say something else, maybe even hold his hand, but I don't.

I want to, more than anything, but the truth is, I don't trust my voice not to crack for the broken boy inside of him. So I watch the city smear past in flashes of red and gold, and pretend, for just a few more seconds, that we're both okay.

———

As the search for Ollie continues, we pass a corner store, and I catch my reflection in the glass. It's just a blur, but it's enough to leave a lasting impression. My eyes are wide. My hands are shaking. It's the same hollow look I thought I'd buried.

For a second, I see her again. The girl caged in the shed. The one who flinched at every sound and never thought she'd make it out. She's still here, still living inside me, still waiting for the world to prove just how cruel it can really be.

I blink the thought away and force myself to focus.

Ollie's out there and Dallas needs me.

"He's probably somewhere familiar," I say, scanning every shadow, every sidewalk. "You always take him to the same places, right?"

Dallas nods, swallowing hard. "Yeah. I do."

I chance a glance at him.

His jaw is clenched and his eyes are darting from street to street.

"The playground," I blurt. "The one by the laundromat. You told me you like to take him there after errands. He loves that place, right?"

Dallas blinks. "Yeah. Yeah, he does."

He swerves the wheel without hesitation and guns it for the playground.

We find him there five minutes later, sitting under the jungle gym, tail wagging, tongue out, completely unaware as he chews on a disgusting-looking stick.

"Ollie!" Dallas shouts.

Ollie perks up, lets out a bark, and barrels straight for us. Dallas drops to his knees and scoops him up, wrapping his arms around him like a lifeline. "Jesus Christ," he mutters, voice thick. "You little asshole. Don't do that again."

He holds Ollie and I can tell he's more than just a dog to him. He's family. Losing him would've taken something irreplaceable from his life. I wonder what it would feel like to be held like that. To be loved like that.

I inch a few feet back, giving them space, but as soon as he spots me, Ollie has other plans. Just as Dallas finishes putting his collar and leash back on, Ollie wriggles free of his arms, races in a wide circle around both of us, and somehow, *somehow*, wraps both of our legs in his leash.

Dallas grabs me by the waist to keep me from falling. We face each other, chest-to-chest, breathing hard. I've regained my balance, but his hands are still wrapped around me, and he hasn't let go.

He swallows and his eyes search mine.

"You found him," he breathes.

His thumb traces the edge of my jaw and I can tell he's holding back everything he isn't ready to say.

Then, he kisses me. It's not tentative like how I kissed Rome. It's desperate and fast, like he's been holding back for too long and now he can't control it.

His hand cups my jaw as my fingers knot in his shirt. There's nothing sweet about the kiss. It's all heat and pressure and months of tension finally snapping loose. I melt into it.

Because this is *Dallas*. Handsome, charming, cocky, infuriating Dallas. Who's so sincere sometimes it hurts.

When we finally pull apart, we're both breathing hard. Ollie barks, like he's proud of himself and I can't help but wonder if this was the plan all along.

Dallas grins, a little sheepishly. "Guess he's a fan of a slow burn."

I smile despite myself.

"Come on," he says, voice warm against my skin. "Let's go home."

EIGHTEEN

VIOLET

The rain starts around dusk. Soft at first. Nothing more than a whisper against the windows. Then it gets heavier. Louder. Until its pounding drowns out everything else.

I don't know where the guys are. Rome said he had paperwork to do. Dallas probably went out somewhere with Ollie. And Niko… well, Niko never really tells anyone what he's doing.

I'm alone in the kitchen, blasting music through my headphones while whisking whipped cream in a half-hearted attempt to drown out the noise in my head.

The beat is loud, the lyrics, numbingly upbeat, but it's not enough. I crank the volume higher and whisk harder, letting the repetitive motion do what it can to distract me.

There were more texts today. Three, maybe four. I didn't open them. Only glanced at the previews before swiping them away. But he sounded *different*. Angrier. I think he could tell I was ignoring him.

So, I threw myself into baking. I told myself it was just a distraction. That I needed to keep my hands busy to stop from checking my phone. But somewhere along the way, the distraction turned into cheesecake - a vanilla bean cheesecake to be exact. *Dallas' favorite.*

I didn't do that on purpose. At least, I don't *think* I did. But maybe, underneath all the noise in my head, some desperate part of me wanted to impress him.

As if that matters. As if winning him over will somehow make up for the fact that I've been hiding things from him. Lying by omission, pretending everything's fine when it's not. It's ridiculous.

How can I want something more with him, with any of them, when I can't even trust them with the truth?

Still, I can't stop thinking about the way he looked at me the other night. The way his mouth tasted.

I always knew Dallas was hot. Anyone with eyes could see that. But now, my attraction to him is so much worse. I know what he smells like up close, what he sounds like when he groans in my ear, and what his hands feel like when they're wrapped around me. It's all so freaking confusing.

———

THE FIRST FLICKER comes just as I finish topping the cheesecake. Then, the lights go out, the refrigerator shuts off, and the room gets swallowed in darkness.

I rip my headphones off and toss them on the counter. For a second, I just stand there, blinking into the sudden dark. Then comes a sound that makes my heart leap out of my chest. Not from the storm, but from something inside.

A bang. A loud one that sounds like someone slamming a fist against the wall.

My stomach drops.

Another bang follows, louder this time. Then, a muffled voice calls out, sharp and frantic.

I grab my phone off the counter, turn on the flashlight,

and move. The hallway stretches ahead and the beam of light shakes as I walk, slicing through the shadows.

"Hello?" I call out, my voice low.

No answer. Just another thud coming from the direction of Niko's room. I reach his door and try to open it, but it doesn't move.

"Niko." I say, pressing my ear to the door. "Are you in there?"

"Vi?"

Relief flows through me. "Yeah."

"I- I can't get the door open. The manual lock is jammed."

I blink, trying to process. His room is the only one in the house with a biometric lock. Something Rome said he insisted on for privacy.

"You're stuck in there?"

"…Yeah."

There's something in his voice I've never heard before. Not from Niko, the man who stares down threats like they bore him. It's panic.

"Hold on," I tell him, already turning on my heel.

I sprint down the hallway, past the darkened living room, into the utility closet. The shadows feel thicker here, closer. I dig past old batteries and cleaning supplies and feel my fingers graze against cold steel. It's the crowbar Rome stashed here weeks ago. "Just in case," he'd said. I never thought we'd have a use for it.

By the time I get back to Niko's door, my chest is tight from more than just running.

"I've got it," I say, jamming the crowbar into the seam between the door and frame. "It's gonna make noise."

I press my shoulder against the door and push. The metal groans and the frame creaks like it's about to snap in half.

"Come on," I mutter under my breath, throwing my weight into it again.

A crack. A pop. Then the door gives way. It swings open

an inch, and I finally see Niko. He's shirtless and pale, with sweat shining across his collarbones and his jaw is clenched tight. His chest is rising and falling rapidly and his eyes are wild and unfocused. I step into the room and his expression still doesn't change. He just stares through me like something else entirely is playing out before him.

"Hey," I say softly.

His eyes shift towards me, but he still doesn't move or speak. His muscles are tightly locked in place and his rapid breathing still hasn't subsided. It doesn't take me long to figure out what's going on with him. Niko is scared of the dark.

———

THE CANDLES FLICKER QUIETLY, casting soft amber light across the room.

The storm's still going outside, wind dragging rain against the windows, but in here, everything feels still. We sit on the floor, shoulder to shoulder, backs to the wall.

Niko hasn't said a word since I opened the door. He's just watching me. His gaze is steady now, but his face is unreadable as ever.

I don't mind the silence, though. Sometimes silence is better than talking. Sometimes it's the only thing that helps. Words ask for explanations. Silence just lets you breathe.

After a while, I shift and push up to my feet. Niko's shoulders tense immediately, his eyes flicking up like he's bracing for something. He thinks I'm going to walk out, going to leave him here alone with the dark.

"Is it okay if I sleep in here tonight?" I ask quietly. "The storm is creeping me out a little."

His expression softens, and the tension in his shoulders eases, just a fraction. "Oh course."

I blow out the candles closest to the floor, strip off my

hoodie, then crawl onto the bed and slip under the blanket. Niko follows a moment later and the mattress dips under his weight.

His arm wraps around me, careful at first. Hesitant, like he's waiting to see if I'll pull away. I don't. I just breathe and relax into his touch. Then, slowly, he pulls me closer, tighter.

His grip is firm, almost desperate, and it feels like if he lets go, something inside him might break open. But I don't mind, and I don't pull away. I get it, he needs me right now, and for once, it feels good to be the one that's needed.

I turn in his arms and press my face against his chest, letting the steady rise and fall of his breathing anchor me. Outside, the storm keeps raging. But in here, in this room filled with candlelight and words left unsaid, something inside me settles. And I realize, maybe I'm not as alone as I thought I was.

NINETEEN

NIKO

THE CANDLES BURNED OUT A WHILE AGO, BUT I'M STILL AWAKE, lying here watching her sleep.

Tonight's attack was intense. Probably the worst I've had in years. I should still be there now. In that hell the dark always drags me to. But she walked in and pulled me out, like she knew exactly how to find me.

She didn't flinch when she saw me shaking. Didn't talk me down or feed me some bullshit about how I was "okay." She just quietly rode out the storm with me.

Now she's sleeping on my chest, with one hand tucked under her cheek, and the other wrapped around my waist like she's making sure I don't disappear on her again.

She's a fucking angel. One I don't deserve. Every breath she takes grounds me in the present. In this bed. In this moment. Not in the dark. Not in *that* house. Not in *that* fucking closet.

Violet shifts in her sleep and settles closer, like she subconsciously sensed I was slipping away again. I brush a strand of purple hair from her face and tuck it behind her ear. I shouldn't touch her like this. I shouldn't look at her like she's mine. *But I do.* Because to me, she already is.

I press a kiss to her forehead, and she stirs, shifting again to press closer. Her thigh hooks over my hip, and it drags the hem of her shorts higher.

"Vi," I breathe, more prayer than warning.

She makes a soft noise. Half sigh, half whimper.Her hips rock into mine, and I feel everything. The pressure, the heat, the fucking pulse of it. This is torture, but it's the kind I'd kneel for.

Her eyes flutter open and she studies my face as she grinds into me again, slow and uncertain, like she's testing the boundary. The friction alone has me seeing stars.

I tighten my hand on her hip, giving her all the answer she needs.Her breath hitches. I feel it in her chest, right against mine. Then she grinds against me again, harder.

Fuck.

My forehead presses into hers. My eyes stay shut. I'm not thinking. I'm just feeling. Her weight against me. Her skin under my hands. The feel of her body against mine through too many layers. I bite back a groan when her hand grips my shoulder for leverage.

It's not sex, but it's fucking close, and in some ways, it's much more intimate. Because it's desperate. Our clothes are on. Our breaths are ragged. There's nothing clean or pretty about it.

I grip her thigh, not to stop her, but to hold her steady. To make sure she knows I'm not going anywhere, that she can take from me, and *fuck*, does she take. She rolls her hips again, firmer this time, right against my cock. The heat of her soaked pussy through her shorts is almost enough to kill me.

My eyes slam shut. My jaw locks. I don't move. Don't thrust. I just let her use me. Because this? This isn't about me, it's about *her*.

"Good girl," I murmur, the word more vibration than sound.

Her breath stutters, then she moans, quiet and strangled, as she grinds down harder.

I feel her everywhere. In the heat seeping through both our clothes. In the way her fingers dig into my shoulder. In the tremble that runs down her spine when she starts to fall apart.

She moves one last time, grinding right against the thick shaft of my cock, and instantly shatters. Her whole body locks up. A low gasp slips from her lips as she comes, and her eyes roll back as she trembles. She buries her face in my chest, and I just hold her. Tighter than I should. I didn't finish, but I don't care, because this, *her*. Wrapped around me like I'm the only thing keeping her grounded?It's everything.

And right now, I don't feel like a killer. Or a ghost. Or a fucking monster. I just feel like *hers*.

TWENTY

VIOLET

I wake up to the sound of steady breathing and the low whir of a fan somewhere overhead. For a second, I forget where I am. Then I feel it. The warmth behind me. The press of a chest against my spine. The rise and fall of Niko's breath at the back of my neck.

His arm is slung across my waist. His palm rests low. Too low. Right over the tattoo. My pulse skips. *I forgot to cover it.*

A cold weight drops into my stomach.

I try not to move, try not to breathe, but I can already feel the panic tightening in my chest. Crawling in slow, itchy spirals underneath my skin.

If he hasn't already, Niko is going to notice it. It's still dark in here, but the lettering is big, inked in thick black lines just below my navel. Written in that monster's handwriting. Slanted. Possessive. *Ugly.*

MINE.

He etched that word into my skin like he owned me. Not like a person, not even like a pet, like a thing.

I can't let Niko see it.

I shift out of bed carefully, sliding out from under his arm, while tugging the hem of my t-shirt down. I grab my hoodie off the floor and slip it over my head.

"Don't go." Niko calls out.

I freeze and turn back to face him. He's sitting up now, hair tousled, eyes heavy with sleep.

"I just need a little air," I lie.

His gaze drops to my hands, to the way they're clenched around the bottom hem of my hoodie. He says nothing for a beat. Then,

"You're worried I saw it. The tattoo."

My breath catches and Niko's eyes hold mine for a long moment. They're unreadable as ever, but it feels like he's sifting through what to say next.

"I did," he says finally.

I close my eyes, shame flooding in like a wave. "It's not what you think."

"It doesn't matter what I think."

I look at him. "Then why did you tell me you saw it?"

He swings his legs off the bed and stands slowly, weighing every word. "Because I know what it's like," he says. "To live with scars that someone else gave you. To have to look in the mirror and see the damage they left behind."

My throat tightens.

"Do you want it gone?"

I stare at him, at the quiet in his expression, at the gentleness of his question. I nod.

"Then let's go."

———

THE TATTOO SHOP IS SMALL, tucked between a Thai restaurant and a boutique bookstore. The windows are dark. The neon sign above the door is off, and the metal gate is drawn. It's closed. *Obviously.*

I shift on my feet and glance at him. "It's okay. We can come back tomorrow."

Niko doesn't answer. Just checks his phone, taps something, and slips it back in his pocket like the matter's already settled.

I'm just about to ask what we're still doing here when headlights sweep across the lot behind us.A motorcycle pulls in and parks right in front of the shop.

The man who swings off it and pulls off his helmet looks like he stepped straight out of an indie rock band. He's wearing a worn button-up flannel, black skinny jeans, and has intricate tattoos crawling from his knuckles all the way up his neck.

His long dark hair's pulled up in a knot, and he has stacks of metal rings adorning both of his hands. He doesn't hesitate when he sees us.

"Sorry for the wait," he says with a grin. "Niko, good to see you, man."

Niko gives him a small nod.

He turns to me next. "I'm Sean, you must be Violet. You ready for some middle-of-the-night ink, or should I put on a pot of coffee first?"

I smile, "Uhh, I think I'm good."

He nods and walks over to unlock the shop door. "Let's get started then. Niko gave me a rundown of the cover and I've got a design in mind that might be perfect, if you're open to it."

He holds the door open and waits until we walk through before following us in.

Sean flips on a switch and low music sounds through the speakers. Something wordless. All ambient synth and distant echoes. He moves with quiet efficiency, setting up his station, laying out tools, snapping on gloves like he's done this a thousand times. I sit on the padded table, legs swinging.

Sean glances up from his tray. "Mind if I take a look?"

I hesitate for a beat, then gather up my shirt and hoodie and pull them up to my chest. I keep my arms crossed over my ribs, hands gripping my elbows as the cold air brushes over my skin.

Sean leans in, inspecting the ink like it's something to solve, not something to judge. Niko doesn't speak either, but I feel his gaze on me, and when I look at him, I catch it. Something in his eyes I can't quite name. It's like sadness mixed with a tinge of anger simmering underneath it. Not at me, *for* me.

"I've been working on something," Sean says, walking over to his desk. "Figured it might suit you, but you tell me if we should change it up."

He flips open a sketchbook and tilts it so I can see. It's a moth with its wings spread wide, etched in delicate lines and laced with soft swirls. It's beautiful. Otherworldly. Quiet but powerful.

"What do you think?"

I nod. "It's gorgeous."

"Want me to add anything to customize it? We can switch out the swirls for something more meaningful to you."

I pause for a moment to think. "Could you maybe add stars to it? I've always been obsessed with the night sky."

Sean gives me a nod. "We'll make it yours."

He works up a stencil and presses the outline to my skin. When he peels the paper back, I stare at the reflection in the mirror he holds up. The word that was once branded there is gone, buried beneath the most majestic wings covered in stars and crescent moons.

"This okay?" He asks.

I nod again, fighting a smile. It's better than okay, *it's perfect.*

I lie down and the buzzing starts, only this time it's not something being taken from me. It's something being reclaimed.

Niko sits in the chair beside me, holding my hand and letting his thumb brush slow circles over my wrist. The tattoo takes three hours to complete. By the time Sean wipes down the last line and wraps my stomach in cling wrap, I feel wrung out and half-drunk on exhaustion. We thank him for his time and he nods like it's no big deal, already cleaning his station.

Niko leads me outside and opens his passenger door for me. I hop inside and he waits until I'm settled before closing the door and rounding the front. I assume we're heading home, but when he slides behind the wheel, he doesn't drive towards the apartment.

Instead, he glances over. "One more place."

There's something about the way he says it that makes questioning him feel unnecessary, like I subconsciously know that whatever road he's taking me down, I'll be okay.

———

WE DRIVE IN SILENCE, the city lights blurring through the windows, until the buildings thin and the air turns cooler.

He pulls off the road and coasts up a winding hill that crests into a flat clearing. And then I see the view.

All of San Francisco sprawled out below us like someone spilled a box of glitter across black velvet. Every window, every streetlamp, every car winding through the hills, become tiny flecks of gold against the night. The sky above is just as dazzling. Wide and open. Stars scattered in thick constellations.

I don't realize I stopped breathing until I let it out in one long exhale. "It's beautiful up here," I whisper.

Niko shifts in his seat and reaches behind us into the cab, pulling out a couple of folded blankets and two pillows.

I arch a brow.

He shrugs, like it's obvious. "For nights when I have to crash between jobs."

He opens the truck bed and hops up, laying everything out with quick, practiced movements. Then he reaches a hand down toward me and I take it. He helps me up, settles me on the blanket, and then lies beside me, close but not pressing.

We lie in silence, side by side in the truck bed, watching the sky shift. The stars are brighter up here. Closer. Like if I reached out, I could pull one down and keep it for myself.

Niko's hand rests in mine, his thumb brushing over my knuckles like it's second nature.

I tilt my head toward him, voice quiet. "Thank you. For tonight."

He says nothing, just turns his head slightly until his eyes meet mine. Niko doesn't need words to make you feel something. His gaze alone does the work and right now, it's locked on me like I'm the only thing in the universe that matters. My whole body heats.

There's no rush, no demand, just this slow, magnetic pull between us that makes me lean in before I even realize I'm moving. I kiss him. Soft at first. Testing. Then deeper. Hotter.

His fingers slip into my hair, and when I moan into his mouth, I feel his body respond. He moves over me, pressing me back against the blanket as his knee slots between my legs and spreads them with quiet authority.

His lips trail down my neck, and when his teeth graze the skin just above my collarbone, I moan, and my hips arch instinctively. He pulls back to look at me, a silent question in his eyes, and I nod my head softly. I want this. I want *him.*

I tug his shirt over his head and run my fingers down the hard lines of his chest. He's solid everywhere. Tense, like he's still trying to hold something back. But I don't want restraint, not from him.

"Niko," I whisper.

His name tastes like sin on my tongue. He kisses me again, slower this time, taking his time to explore my mouth.

Then his hand dips below the waistband of my shorts. One finger. Then two. Slipping through my wetness with agonizing precision.

I arch, gasping as he slowly circles my clit.

"You're so soaked for me," he murmurs, his voice rough in my ear. "Fuck, Vi. Should I stop?"

"No," I breathe. "I don't want you to stop."

That's all it takes. He sits back just long enough to drag my shorts down my legs, tossing them somewhere in the truck bed. I reach for his belt, fumbling with the buckle, but he bats my hands away with a smirk and undoes it himself, watching me the whole time.

His cock springs free. Thick, hard, and flushed at the tip. He slips a condom on, and my core aches, like it already knows what's coming. But before I can move, he's already lowering himself over me again, lining himself up with practiced ease. And then he slides inside.

The stretch is brutal. Too much and perfect all at once. I dig my nails into his back, mouth falling open as he fills me slowly, giving me every inch. He groans, deep and guttural, as my walls clench around him, and reaches for my hand.

"Fuck," he hisses, pinning my hand above my head as our fingers intertwine. "You feel like heaven."

He starts to move. Slow, deep strokes that make my whole body tremble. I wrap my legs around his waist, urging him deeper, harder. Every thrust sends sparks ricocheting up my spine. The cool night air drifts over my overheated skin, and the stars blur behind him, turning him into a shadow moving only for me.

Niko doesn't let go of my hand. Even as he fucks me harder, even as I cry out beneath him, begging for more, he keeps our fingers locked. Tethered. Grounded.

His other hand slides between us, thumb finding my clit

and rubbing tight, relentless circles that send me spiraling. I clench around him, gasping as my orgasm hits. It tears through me like wildfire. Searing, sweet, and all-consuming.

I cry out his name, back arching, legs trembling. Niko growls low in his throat, driving into me one last time before he spills inside with a stuttered groan, and collapses against me.

For a long moment, neither of us speaks. We just lay there with our bodies pressed together and our hearts beating in sync. The wind picks up, brushing cool air across our over-heated skin. I shift beneath him, and Niko grunts softly, lifting himself just enough to grab the blanket and tug it over us.

His body is still pressed against mine, but it's not the sex that has my heart warming. It's the way he doesn't pull away. Doesn't rush to fix his clothes or build his walls back up. He just rests his forehead against mine and peppers kisses all over my face.

We lie like that for a while, hearts slowing, skin slick and tangled.

"That tattoo made me feel like I didn't own my body anymore." I murmur. "Thank you. For everything."

"If it matters to you, it matters to me." He says, lifting our still-joined hands and pressing a kiss to my knuckles. Somehow, it feels more intimate than everything else we did tonight.

We stay wrapped up in each other beneath the stars, the whole world quiet for once. Just us. No fear, no guilt, no past clawing at the edges. Only this moment and the guy who held my hand the whole way through it.

TWENTY-ONE

VIOLET

It's been two days and my moth tattoo still looks fresh enough to fly off my skin. The edges are sharp, the fine lines are clean, and every little detail is perfect. I run my fingertips over the ink and smirk.

I can't believe I actually did it.

I look up and catch Niko standing in the doorway, leaning against it and I mindlessly wonder how long he's been watching me.

His eyes land on my stomach. "How's it healing?"

"Good, I think." I say, lifting the hem of my shirt higher.

He pushes off the doorframe and stands in front of me to get a better look. His fingertips trail across the curves of my lower stomach and skim the edge of the tattoo. His touch is light, careful, but it sparks heat deep in belly.

"Looks good." He says, his voice low. "Healing fast."

I swallow and smooth the fabric back down.

There has to be something wrong with me.

Ever since we hooked up, it's like I notice every little thing he does now. Every touch. Every gaze. Every smile meant just for me. All of it sends my heart rate skyrocketing.

It wouldn't be as embarrassing if I knew he felt the same, but I don't know how he feels because we haven't talked about it yet. Not when we passed each other in the kitchen yesterday morning. Not when watched T.V. together last night. Now he's standing here, smelling good, looking dangerously beautiful as ever, and my brain is completely stalling out around him.

"Something's on your mind," he says, like he's pulling the thought straight out of my head.

I force a shrug. "Not really."

He moves before I can blink. One second there's space between us, the next my back is pressed against the wall. Not hard, but enough to feel the message in it.

He plants both hands on either side of my head, caging me in like a wild animal.

"What is it?" He asks, though it feels more like a demand than a question.

My pulse spikes. "Nothing."

His eyes narrow, and he cocks his head. "Try again."

I look anywhere but at him, the floor, the hallway, the fine hair along his muscular forearm. "It's… about the other night."

His gaze sharpens. "Go on."

I swallow hard. "I just don't know what it meant… to you."

For a moment, he studies me and I wonder if he's deciding if I can handle the truth. Then his left hand slides down and settles over my hip.

"It meant," he says, leaning in until his mouth is a breath from my ear, "exactly what you think it did."

My mouth goes dry, and I blink up at him. "And what exactly is that?"

He clenches his jaw. "You tell me."

I frown, ready to tell him I asked first, but he cuts me off by leaning in closer, so close that his minty breath fans across my cheeks.

"I'm in," he says, the words low and certain. "I want you. All of you. Only you."

His gaze locks on mine, steady and unflinching. I want to match him. I want to say something just as solid, just as sure, but my head trips over the words before I can find them. Because "only you" would be a lie. Dallas and Rome are tangled in there too.

My brow furrows as my mouth opens, then shuts again.

"Relax, Vi," he says quietly. "I'm not expecting a response. I just wanted you to know where I stand."

He studies me for another beat, like he's making sure the words sank in, then he pushes off the wall and heads for the door.

"Niko... wait." I say, flustered. "I-"

He turns back to look at me just as he crosses the threshold. "Don't worry, I'm not going anywhere. You're it for me, Violet Warner. Take all the time you need; I'll be here when you're ready or even if you're not."

The door clicks shut behind him, but his words don't follow. They linger in the air, heavy and impossible to ignore.

You're it for me. It should feel like too much. Like something that pins me down and suffocates me. But it makes my chest warm in the best and worst ways.

I want to believe him. I want to believe there's a world where I can be his and still be Dallas's and Rome's too. But wanting and having aren't the same thing.

I press my hands to the wall, trying to ground myself in the solid weight of it. The sting of the tattoo is still there beneath my shirt. A gentle reminder that not all pain is bad. That some things are worth feeling, even when they scare you. And maybe, just maybe, this is one of them.

TWENTY-TWO

VIOLET

I'M IN THE KITCHEN WHEN I HEAR THE ELEVATOR. THE SOFT mechanical sound of it approaching is subtle at first. So quiet it barely registers over the simmering water on the stove. But then it dings, and the sound hits like a gunshot in my chest. My body stills.

The guys are out on a mission. No one should be coming up. Not without a keycard. Not unless...

My heart slams against my ribs as my brain fills in the worst-case scenario.

He found me.

I flick off the stove, grab the biggest knife from the block, and crouch low behind the kitchen island.

Thank God, Ollie's fast asleep in his crate.

Footsteps echo down the hallway, and my breath hitches. They're slow, steady, and getting closer. I press myself tighter to the cabinets and clench my fists, knife braced and ready. The moment the footsteps are close enough, I spring up, ready to attack.

"Jesus!" Dallas jumps, his hand instinctively raising in defense.

My knife stops mid-air.

I take him in. The dimples, the golden tan, the familiar weight of his stare and the panic drains just enough for my hands to stop shaking.

"Well, hey there, psycho Barbie."

I stare, panting, still not lowering the blade.

Dallas lifts both hands in surrender. "Look, if this is about me finishing the last of your mochi, I *swear* it wasn't on purpose."

My hand drops. So does the knife. I let out a breath that turns into a half-laugh, half-sob. "What the hell are you doing here?"

He steps forward slowly, like he's approaching a spooked animal. "The job only needed two of us on-site. We drew straws to see who got to come home to you. Clearly the best man won."

He smiles, but I can see the flicker of concern in his eyes.

"You okay?" he asks.

I nod. Then shake my head. Then nod again.

His brows lift. "So is that a yes and a no?"

"I thought-" I exhale hard. "Never mind."

"You thought it was another attacker," he says, voice softer now.

Dallas' jaw tightens, just for a second. Then he steps closer and nudges the knife away with his boot. "Well, the good news is, I'm home and we're having a movie date tonight. The bad news is, I'm dangerously handsome, and come bearing snacks, which, as you know, is your kryptonite."

He tosses a plastic bag at me. It's filled with sour watermelon gummies, chocolate-covered raisins, and peanut butter M&M's.

I blink down at the candy. "How did you remember all of my favorite movie snacks?"

Dallas shrugs and offers me a smile. "I pay attention, V. Especially when it comes to you."

Dallas heads into the kitchen to grab us drinks while I recover on the couch, trying to calm my still-jittering nerves.

"I already have the perfect movie picked out." He calls out, peeking his head out of the fridge.

I arch a brow. "You sure I'm going to like it? You know I have a discerning taste."

"Please," he grins, settling beside me with two bottles of water and the remote in hand, "I've had this cued up for weeks."

The title appears on the screen. K-Pop Demon Hunters. And I laugh despite myself. It is *exactly* the kind of movie I'd watch.

––––

WE'RE ALMOST DONE with the movie when it happens. The part I didn't know to brace for. The part I didn't see coming.

The quiet, broody love interest, the only person who ever looked at the main girl like she wasn't damaged, throws himself in front of the demon king's fire to protect her. And after a few heartbreaking seconds, he's gone.

It guts me, and suddenly I'm crying. Silently. Shamefully. I sink deeper into the blanket, hoping I can hide it my tears if I just shift the fabric high enough. Dallas notices.

"Hey." He leans in. "What's wrong?"

I shake my head. "Nothing. It's stupid. I'm fine. I just didn't expect that. I thought they'd get a happy ending."

He studies my face for a second before brushing a tear off my cheek with his thumb. He's not trying to fix it. Not trying to put a Band-Aid on it. He's just letting me feel and doing what he can to help me through it.

"It's just a movie," I try to say, but my voice cracks on the words.

Another tear slips free. Dallas leans in and kisses it away. Then another. And another.

He doesn't ask what's wrong. He just keeps kissing every tear like it matters. Like I matter. And when our lips finally meet, I let them. Because tonight, I need to believe in someone who sees all my cracks and stays anyway.

His kiss feels soft, reverent, like I'm something fragile he's scared to break. My world narrows to the feel of his mouth, to the weight of his hand as it grips onto my hair, and to the heat blooming low in my belly as he shifts closer.

He moves like he's dreamed of this a thousand times. Like every stroke of his hand is a promise he's been dying to keep. His hand slides between my legs dragging up the inside of my thigh, slow and patient and possessive. I gasp into his mouth when his fingers graze the edge of my panties.

"I've wanted this," he says, voice rough. "But I didn't want to push."

"You're not," I breathe.

"Tell me to stop."

"I won't."

Dallas flashes me a mischievous grin, like I've just bared my throat to a wolf and dared him to take a bite.

"Feel that?" he murmurs, dragging his thumb across my slick seam. "That's how bad you need me."

He lifts me effortlessly, settling me into his lap so we're sitting face to face. His mouth trails down my neck, teeth grazing skin that feels too hot, too exposed. I whimper when he sucks gently, leaving a mark. My hips grind against his instinctively, and he groans low in his throat.

"Fuck, you feel so good already," he mutters. "So warm. So perfect. I need to be inside of you."

I tug his shirt up and over his head, and splay my hands across his golden chest, tracing the lines of muscle and heat. His hands grip my waist, and he thrusts his hips, cock straining against his sweats beneath me.

My whole body aches from the feel of him.

He pulls off my shirt, leaving me in nothing but a bralette and boy shorts and his eyes rake over me like I'm a wish he's finally been granted. I reach for his waistband, and he lifts me off of his lap to help me free him.

He slips a condom on and then I feel him, thick, hard, and ready. I slide my panties off, climb on his lap again, and sink onto him, inch by delicious inch. Dallas groans as his head falls back.

"Fuck, V."

My eyes flutter shut as I move. Slow at first. Grinding in steady waves until he's moaning my name like it's the only word he knows. His hands tighten on my hips, guiding the pace. I brace my hands on his shoulders and ride him harder, chasing the heat building inside me.

"Look at me," he says, voice hoarse. "I want to watch you when you come apart on my cock."

I meet his eyes as the pressure explodes inside me, as my walls clench tight and my whole body trembles. He follows me over the edge with a broken groan, holding me close as his own release rakes through him.

We don't speak for a long time. We just lie there on the couch, breathing slowly. Eventually, the movie ends and the credits roll.

I curl into his side and press my cheek to his chest, listening to the slow rhythm of his heartbeat. The screen fades to black, and the room dims.

"I didn't think the movie would end like that," I whisper.

Dallas's voice is low and tired. "I kinda did."

I tilt my head to glance up at him. "Why?"

He shrugs, mouth curved in the faintest smile. "Damaged girl. Tragic love. It's the kind of story people like to write."

"Yeah," I say. "But I still hoped."

He pulls me in tighter, tucking my head under his chin. "Me too, V. Me too."

Eventually, the quiet lulls us to sleep. My breathing slows, and somewhere between the weight of his arm around me and the warmth of his body, I stop waiting for the other shoe to drop.

TWENTY-THREE

DALLAS

I WAKE UP, AND THE FIRST THING THAT REGISTERS IS THE stiffness in my neck. *Damn couch sleep.* I crack my eyes open, squint at the morning light bleeding in through the windows, and take a quick look around. The living room is quiet, V's blanket's on the floor, and my arm is draped over the spot where she used to be.

For a second, I worry she ran. That she snuck off while I was sleeping because she regretted what happened. Then I hear the faint pad of her footsteps coming down the hall.

I push up, scrubbing a hand through my hair, and she appears. Freshly showered, barefoot, wearing a matching t-shirt and short set, with her hair twisted up in a loose knot.

"Morning, Darlin'. Where'd you run off to?" I ask, voice still rough from sleep.

Her gaze flicks to me, quick and almost guilty. "I woke up around midnight and ended up crashing in my room. I... figured the guys would come home eventually, and I didn't want them to find us like that."

I grin before I can stop myself. "Like that, huh?"

She rolls her eyes, but there's a blush creeping up her neck. It's cute. *Hell,* it's more than cute. It's adorable.

She's worried they'd be jealous, or pissed, or judge her for last night. Like we all don't already know she has every single one of us tied up in knots.

"Coffee?" she asks, already heading for the kitchen.

I follow, leaning against the doorway while she pours a cup and slides it across the counter to me. She hesitates, just for a breath, but it's long enough for me to know something's on her mind.

"I, um…" She shifts the mug in her hands. "I'm hooking up with Niko, and I've also kissed Rome."

She says it like she's bracing for an explosion.

I take a slow sip of my coffee and look at her. "Okay."

"I should've told you sooner," she rushes, eyes darting up to mine. "It started a couple of weeks ago, but I just, I didn't expect…" She sighs. "I don't want to come between the three of you, and *God,* what the hell am I even doing-"

"V." I set my mug down, stepping close enough to smell the faint vanilla of her shampoo. "I don't own you. None of us do. Niko's one of my best friends. So is Rome. If you make them happy, why the hell would I be mad or wanna take that away from them?"

She looks at me like I've just spoken in a language she doesn't understand. "I just… didn't think you'd be okay with it."

A new voice cuts in from the hall.

"He's right, you know."

We both turn to find Niko standing in the hall, with his black t-shirt rumpled and his eyes locked on her. Her blush deepens, and her gaze drops to her feet.

He steps into the kitchen to join us. "I won't lie. Sharing doesn't come naturally to me. But you're not a possession, Vi; you're a person. And I can't be mad that your heart has room for more than one of us in it."

Her brow furrows and her lips part like she wants to say something, but no words come out. She fidgets with the hem of her shirt, eyes bouncing between us like she's not sure which direction is safer to look at.

"Are you sure?" She says, exasperated. "I don't want to mess this up."

"Mess what up?" Rome asks, wandering out of his room. He looks half awake, and his dark hair is sticking up all over the place, like he fought with his pillow last night and lost.

Violet's eyes go wide, and she visibly swallows. "Nothing. I… uh-" She scrambles for her coffee mug and lifts it in the air. "I'm just gonna go drink this in my room."

She disappears down the hall without another word and slides her door shut.

Rome arches a brow. "Was it something I said?"

I take another slow sip of my coffee, hiding my smirk.

"What?" He asks, looking between me and Niko. "What did I miss?"

I lift my arms in a lazy stretch and yawn.

"V's freaking out because we're all secretly in love with her and are probably going to go full alpha asshole mode on each other if she doesn't choose one of us."

Rome's eyes flare. "That's not… I would never ask her to-"

"Relax, big boy." I say, patting him on the shoulder with a smile. "We told her she didn't have to choose. Now, sit down and grab some breakfast."

Rome breathes a sigh of relief. Niko's mouth twitches like he's fighting a smile. And I take another sip of my coffee and daydream about the girl that fell asleep wrapped in my arms last night.

TWENTY-FOUR

ROME

THE BURN OF THE WHISKEY HITS FIRST. SHARP, CLEAN, AND JUST shy of punishing as it slides down my throat. It settles low, warm in my gut.

It's late, well past midnight, and everyone else has already sequestered themselves in their rooms. Not me, though. I'm out on the balcony, drink in hand, staring out at the glittering skyline like it might have the answer to fix the mess that's become my life.

I let Violet kiss me. And worse, I kissed her back. I told myself not to cross that line. Told myself it was too dangerous. Too messy. Especially now, while she's under our roof, trusting us to keep her safe. But when she leaned in and I felt the soft press of her lips against mine, every rule I swore I'd follow fucking incinerated.

I hate that I let it happen; I hate that I wanted it, and I hate that, even now, I still want more.

I run my fingers through my hair and tug on the strands, *hard*, like the pain will distract me from my thoughts. I even bought her a bracelet that night. I don't know why the hell I did it. *No*, that's a lie. I know exactly why.

The vendor told me it was meant to protect someone. That you're supposed to give it to the person you care about most. And she was the first person who popped into my mind.

I didn't buy it to impress her; I didn't even expect her to wear it, but she slipped it on without hesitation and hasn't taken it off since. The selfish prick in me likes to think that means something. And who am I to crush his dreams?

I take another sip, slower this time, and let the burn of the whisky remind me that nothing worth having comes without a price.

———

I'M on my second drink when I hear movement inside the apartment. The kitchen lights are on, and Violet's at the counter with her sleeves pushed up, working on something with that ridiculous level of focus she gets when she's baking.

She reaches for a canister of powdered sugar, and the hem of her shirt rides up just enough to flash a strip of soft tan skin.

I should look away. I don't. My phone buzzes on the table beside me. *It's Stevie.* I let it ring out, then flip the screen face-down without checking the message. That's the third time I've done that today. Fourth, if you count the text I ignored last night.

I rub the back of my neck, trying to shake the tension. Stevie knows something's going on. *She has to.* It's like she senses I'm circling something I shouldn't be, and she's absolutely right.

If I were smarter, I'd call her back. Set boundaries. End this now before it gets worse. But instead, I watch her little sister.

Violet turns to grab something, and there's a smear of

white powder across her cheek. *Of course* she has something on her face. She's messy, easily distracted, and effortlessly warm. A walking contradiction to everything I am. Soft where I'm sharp, unpredictable where I'm rigid, and vibrant where I prefer clean lines and silence. She doesn't belong in my world, and yet here she is, bleeding light into everything she touches, including me.

I tell myself to look away. To go back to reminding myself why I don't get involved, why I don't let my guard down. But then poof. The mixer kicks on and powdered sugar goes flying everywhere, covering every inch of her like she's some kind of walking temptation wrapped in sweetness and sin.

Christ.

She swipes her tongue over the dusting of sugar on her lips. Slow and absentmindedly. She has no clue she's lighting a match inside my fucking chest. That's it. *Fuck it.*

I slam my drink down and push off my chair so fast, it slams into the glass railing behind me. I don't even pause to think as I stride toward the kitchen, heat climbing my spine, something reckless sparking under my skin. I'm going to burn when all this shit hits the fan, anyway. Might as well enjoy the fire.

TWENTY-FIVE

VIOLET

I KILL THE MIXER AND COUGH AS A PUFF OF POWDERED SUGAR explodes into the air around me. My face is a mess. The counter's worse. I probably look like I crashed into a bakery.

I reach for a kitchen towel, muttering under my breath. "Okay, yeah… maybe add the milk before you mix the sugar next time."

I'm just about to clean when I hear it. The heavy thud of footsteps. Fast. Purposeful. I turn, expecting to see Dallas, or maybe Niko, awakened by the noise. But it's neither of them. It's Rome. And he looks… *wild.*

His chest is rising, his jaw is tight, and his eyes are burning like I've never seen them before. He's already moving toward me, heat rolling off him in waves. There's something in his expression I can't name, something dangerous and hungry and completely untethered.

"Rome?" I ask, my voice catching in my throat. "I was just baking- sorry about the mess, I'll clean it-"

He shakes his head once. Sharp. Final. And then he's on me. I don't even get the chance to take a step back. His mouth crashes onto mine, hot and demanding, and I gasp as his hands grip tightly around my waist.

My back hits the kitchen island with a thud and I feel the cool granite against my skin as Rome's body presses into mine, all hard muscle and searing heat.

He kisses like he's starving. Like he's been holding back for too long and something inside him finally snapped. I whimper when his tongue sweeps into my mouth, when his teeth graze my bottom lip like he wants to mark me from the inside out.

"You have no idea," he growls against my mouth, "what you do to me."

His hands slide under my thighs, lifting me like I weigh nothing, setting me on the edge of the counter. Powdered sugar sticks to my legs, my arms, his skin. He doesn't care. He licks it off of me like it's holy.

His mouth drags down my neck, rough and wet, and I tilt my head to give him more, my body already shaking from the intensity.

"You smell like vanilla," he groans, voice ragged. "Fuck, of course you do."

I claw at his shirt, desperate to feel his skin. He pulls it off in one fluid motion and tosses it across the room. His hands find the waistband of my shorts and yank them down. My panties follow, ripped halfway, the fabric stretching before giving way.

I gasp. "Rome-"

"Do you want this?" He asks, going eerily still.

I stare into his eyes and feel something low and hot bloom in my stomach. "Yes."

That's all it takes. He picks me up, spins me around, and bends me over the island, one hand fisting in my hair, the other dragging down my spine until I'm arching into him.

"Look at you," he grits out. "Covered in sugar. So fucking sweet. So fucking *mine*."

He pulls his cock free and thrusts into me in one hard, punishing stroke. I cry out, my hands scrambling for purchase against the countertop as he drives into me again. And again. The edge of the island digs into my hips, but I don't care. I want the pain. I want the pleasure. I want *him*.

Every thrust feels like a claim, like he's marking me from the inside out. He leans over my back, tongue licking up my neck as he grinds deep.

"You think I haven't noticed?" he growls. "Every time you walk into a room. Every time you smile at someone else. You're driving me fucking insane."

I moan, too far gone to answer. My legs are shaking, slick with sweat and sugar and want. His hand moves between my legs, fingers finding my clit, rubbing hard, fast, in time with his thrusts.

"Come for me," he commands. "Right now. All over my cock, Violet."

And I do. My body seizes, and a scream tears from my throat as I shatter around him, muscles clenching, vision going white. He follows with a curse and a groan, spilling inside me as he buries himself to the hilt, both of us gasping, trembling.

I don't speak, I can't, not yet. I just stay there, wrecked, with his chest pressed to my back and our bodies still joined.

In the quiet that follows, the only sound is our breathing. Ragged, shallow, and *real*. Then he shifts behind me. I expect him to pull away, to leave me standing here, bent over the counter, ruined and shaking. Instead, his arms wrap around me from behind, lifting me up like I weigh nothing.

"Rome-"

"Don't." His voice is low, possessive, final. "I'm not done with you."

He carries me out of the kitchen like a man possessed. No towel. No clothes. Just powdered sugar on my chest, his cum dripping down my thigh, and his arms locked tight around me like I'm something precious he's stolen and has no intention of giving back.

The air shifts as we pass down the hall. Cooler, quieter, darker. My head rests against his shoulder, but my heart is racing, every nerve still raw and alive.

When we reach his room, he kicks the door open and strides inside without hesitation. And I know, whatever just happened in that kitchen? Was just the beginning.

TWENTY-SIX

ROME

She's asleep on my chest, and I'm not sure I remember how to breathe. Her leg is hooked over mine, one arm draped lazily across my stomach, breath warm against my skin. The bracelet I bought her is still looped around her wrist, smudged with powdered sugar and sweat.

I should be thinking about consequences. About lines crossed, about what this means, but all I can think about is how goddamn *right* she feels here. In my bed. Wrapped around me like she belongs. And maybe that's the problem. Because I've never wanted anything to belong to me more.

I fucked her all night. On the island, against the wall, in the shower, on this bed. We only stopped once the sugar was all gone and her eyes started fluttering shut mid-kiss. Even then, I had to pull her against me and hold her tight, like my body didn't accept that it was over.

She wore me down in the softest, sweetest, filthiest way possible. And now she's here, asleep in my arms like it's the most natural thing in the world.

I stare down at her face, lips parted slightly, lashes sweeping her cheeks, powdered sugar still faintly dusting the lavender hair at her temple. My chest cracks wide open. No excuses, no denial, no carefully structured logic. I fucking love her.

There. It's out. Silent and earth-shattering. Settling in my bones like it's always been there, just waiting for me to admit it. And for once, I don't care about what comes next.

Not about Stevie and The Reapers. Not about the repercussions. Not about how badly I've fucked every rule I've ever lived by. If this comes with fallout, I'll take it. Because she's worth every second of it.

———

MY PHONE BUZZES on the nightstand. I reach for it with one arm, careful not to shift her weight off me. It's a text from Bobby, one of the building's night guards.

Sorry to contact you so late, Mr. Creed. There's a young couple here. Neither will hand over their IDs. But the woman says if we don't let her through, she'll burn down the building.

I sit up just enough to glance at the monitor across the room, with the camera feed already pulled up. It's Stevie and Atlas. *Fuck.*

We all agreed. No visits. No contact. No risks. Them showing up out of nowhere is a problem.

I slip out of bed, tug on a shirt and sweats, and head straight for the elevator. The moment the elevator doors glide open, I step into the lobby and spot Stevie arguing with Bobby, one of the night guards. Atlas stands a few feet behind her, arms crossed, expression unreadable.

"They weren't on the list," Bobby says, throwing me a panicked look. "We told her we can't just-"

"It's fine," I cut in. "They're with me."

The guards step back immediately. "Sorry about that, miss."

Stevie doesn't even glance at them. She turns on me instead, eyes blazing.

"What the fuck, Rome? Why are you ignoring my calls?"

"Hi to you, too." I mutter. "You're looking well."

"We had rules."

"Indeed, we did. Care to explain what you're doing here?"

Stevie narrows her eyes just as Atlas steps between us to interject, "Maybe we should take this somewhere more private."

I exhale through my nose and gesture for them to follow me. "Let's head to my home office."

No one speaks during the ride up, but Stevie doesn't need words. The tension is practically pouring off of her. We make it to the office, and as soon as I shut the door, Stevie lays into me.

"What's going on between you and my sister?"

I should lie, I should deflect, I should make it sound like less than what it is. But I can't, not after what just happened.

"Nothing you need to be concerned about." I say, glancing at Atlas. He's leaning against the wall, watching us and I get the feeling he already knows how this is going to play out.

"Don't bullshit me." Her voice is low, but it cuts sharply. I clench my jaw. "You're crossing a line." She hisses. "Tell me I'm wrong."

I say nothing.

Her glare sharpens. "This was supposed to be temporary. She's here to be safe. Not to play house with three guys who clearly don't know what the fuck they're doing."

Her accusation stings. Yes, things have gotten complicated, but Violet has always been safe with us. We would never let anything bad happen to her.

I shake my head. "She's not some fragile little-"

"Yes, she is," Stevie hisses. "You, of all people, should know that. You saw her, Rome. In that shed. You know what she went through. She's vulnerable, and you let this happen."

"I didn't *let* anything happen. I didn't plan for this. I didn't plan to fall-"

"Don't say it." She says, cutting me off. "Don't you dare say it."

"And if it's the truth?" I ask.

"It better not be." She says sincerely. "Because if it is, when she finds out you've been lying to her, you're going to break her fucking heart."

"That's the last thing I would do." I snap, louder than I mean to.

Atlas steps forward, but Stevie presses a hand against his chest as she turns to face me. "Then you need to be honest. With yourself and with her. If you break her again, there is no coming back from it."

She glances at Atlas, who nods once, and then looks back at me. "Call Dallas and Niko in."

I hesitate, just for a beat. Stevie stares me down. Atlas watches us like he's already planned five outcomes and none end well for me.

"I'm not leaving until I talk to all of you," she says, tilting her chin up.

Shaking my head, I pull out my phone and text the group chat. The reply is instantaneous.

Niko walks in first, sharp-eyed and stone-faced, fully dressed like he never planned on sleeping. Dallas shows up a minute later, barefoot and shirtless in his boxer briefs. His hair is sticking up in every direction, and his eyes are half open. Both of them freeze when they see Stevie.

Dallas squints. "Is this a dream? Please tell me this is a dream."

Atlas smirks. "Nope. It's your fucking intervention."

"I want the truth." Stevie says, folding her arms across her chest. "All of it. Every kiss. Every touch. Every time you crossed a line. I want to know exactly what's been going on between the three of you and my sister. And don't even think about sugarcoating it."

TWENTY-SEVEN

VIOLET

My heart slams into my stomach as the lights above me flicker on and I instantly move into action.

Rummaging for the makeshift weapon I slid under the mattress, I grasp it in my palm, tuck myself into the darkest corner of the bed, and ready myself for what's coming.

The seconds it takes for him to unchain the flimsy metal doors feel like hours, and by the time they swing open and his frame steps into view, adrenaline is coursing through my veins and my heart is practically leaping out of my chest.

His vacant brown eyes scan the room, and when they finally land on me, my whole body trembles.

"There she is." He croons, stepping towards me as he loosens the expensive silk tie around his neck. "My perfect girl. Did you miss me?"

He says it like we mean something to each other. Like I'm not just something he bought and broke over and over again.

I narrow my eyes as he closes the distance between us, tracking his every move. As he draws closer, my eyes catch a tiny beam of light gleaming from the ground in front of him, and my stomach sinks.

Shit.

Its glass. From the skylight I shattered to forge my makeshift weapon. I thought I cleared it all, but in the darkness, I must have missed a piece.

Fuck.

Time slows down, and I watch with bated breath as his shoe hovers over the shard of glass and crunches down on it. His ankle wobbles, and his expression drops. The silence that fills the 10x10 shed is deafening.

He lifts his shoe and looks at the bottom before narrowing his eyes at me. "What is this?"

"I don't know." I breathe.

He cranes his leathery neck to look up at the ceiling.

Do it. I beg myself. Slash his throat now, before he realizes what's happening. I scream at my body to move. To do something. To do anything. But I'm completely frozen in fear, and my muscles are painfully locked into place.

"It's glass." He says, clenching his jaw as he lowers his gaze to look at me.

Cogs turn in his head, and he quickly shifts his focus to the hand I'm hiding behind my back. "What do you have there?"

I swallow the lump in my throat and shake my head. "Nothing."

"Show it to me." He demands through gritted teeth. "Now."

I should refuse. I should attack and fight like hell to get out of here. If I were anything like my older sister, Stevie, I would. But I'm not brave like her. I never have been. And angering him will only make things worse for me.

I jerk my trembling arm forward and pry my hand open, exposing the 4-inch shard of glass.

He lunges towards me in a fury, rips it from my hand and throws it hard against the floor, shattering it into a million pieces. I stare at the fragments, too stunned to move, as he starts to pace.

"I can't believe you thought about betraying me like this." He says, squeezing his eyes shut as he clenches his fists. "You were going to hurt me?" He sneers. "After everything I've done for you?"

His rage is palpable, suffocating me as I curl in on myself to stop my body from shaking. His hand shoots out, gripping my jaw in a bruising hold as he forces me to meet his gaze.

The scent of his pungent cologne assaults my senses as he leans in close. "You are mine." He hisses, his words a menacing promise. "And you always will be. Now, be a good girl and lie down."

My stomach twists at his words.

No. "I said, lie down!" He snaps, furiously unbuttoning his dress shirt to expose his bloated belly.

I choke back the bile crawling up my throat and numbly press myself flat against the filthy mattress.

After a few tense moments of fighting the tremors vibrating through my bones, the mattress dips, and he settles his weight on top of me.

I know what comes next, so I detach myself from my body and allow my mind to float off as I stare up at the broken skylight. Into a place where his grunts are nothing more than whispers in the wind. Into a realm where his touch can't reach me.Into a world where my innocence isn't gone.

My body jerks upright. I blink hard, trying to make sense of where I am. The ceiling is smooth. Whole. The mattress isn't stained. The walls aren't metal.

It's Rome's room. *I'm safe.* I repeat the words to myself like a prayer.

You're safe. You're safe. You're safe.

Something nudges my arm. I flinch, then freeze. A warm snout presses gently against my wrist and I blink down to find Ollie staring up at me, his wide brown eyes filled with worry.

He lets out a soft whine and crawls closer on the bed, burying his head beneath my arm like he's trying to shield me from whatever I saw in the dark.

My face softens. "Hey, Ollie Ollie Oxen Free." My voice is raw. "What are you doing in Rome's room?"

I run my fingers through his golden fur, grateful for the anchor, for the steady weight of something real. He's soft, solid, and warm.

My heart finally begins to settle, each beat thudding slower beneath my ribs. I press a kiss to the top of his head and close my eyes for a second longer, letting his warmth chase the nightmare back into its corner. But then I hear them. Voices. Low, urgent, and real.

My eyes snap open and I see Ollie's ears perk up. I glance at the clock. 1:46 a.m. Way too late for a casual conversation.

I slip out of bed, careful not to jostle Ollie too much, but he hops down behind me anyway, keeping his body glued to mine like he knows I need him.

The voices grow clearer as we step into the hallway. Still muffled, still low, but sharper now, like whoever's talking is angry, but doesn't want to be overheard.

Something's wrong.

Ollie nudges my leg again, almost like he can sense the shift too. We move together toward the sounds and stop just before the doorway to the office. The door isn't fully shut; it's cracked enough so that the sounds slip through.

I hear Rome first. His voice is low and inflectionless. "You're being ridiculous."

"And you don't think you are?" A feminine voice snaps back.

Recognition clicks and my body goes still.

It's my sister. What the hell is she doing here, and why didn't any of them wake me?

"Violet is a grown woman. She's capable of making her own decisions."

"Rome," Stevie says, her tone sharp and unamused. "You can't be serious right now. She isn't in the right mental state; she hasn't been since you met her."

I curl my fingers into fists, squeezing so hard it feels like my bones might splinter. A beat of silence. Then Dallas speaks, voice rough, like he's been woken up but doesn't want to sound careless. "We're not taking advantage of her. If anything, we've been trying to keep our distance. V is... fragile. We all know that."

Fragile. Like I'm a porcelain doll seconds from falling off the shelf and shattering.

Niko's voice cuts through next. Clipped. Defensive. "She's been through a lot. That's not something we take lightly."

"We're just trying to look out for her." Rome adds.

Stevie sighs. "She needs protection. Not whatever *this* is," she snaps. "And if you can't give her that without complicating it, then maybe she shouldn't be here."

The silence that follows is suffocating. I can feel it swelling behind the door.

Rome's voice comes again, quiet, tired. "We get that you're concerned, but Violet is her own person with her own feelings. You can't expect us to just avoid her."

My throat loosens a little. My sister is intense, but at least he's trying to stand up for me.

"You're being paid to keep her safe. Not to get attached."

I stop breathing. The word stabs into my chest like a blade, and twists. *Paid.*

The ground splinters underneath me and I'm suddenly on that frozen lake again. Only now there's no chance of getting to shore. The cracks are spreading fast, and all I can do is wait for the icy water to pull me under.

They're being paid.

I thought I was here because they cared, because they wanted to protect me, because maybe, just maybe, I mattered to them. But no. I'm a job. *A fucking paycheck.* An obligation passed from one hand to another.

My chest caves in, collapsing under the weight of the words. Stevie keeps talking, but I don't wait to hear the rest. I turn and walk away, fast, my bare feet silent against the hard-wood. Ollie scrambles to keep up, but I don't slow down until I make it to my room.

I shut the door behind me, and sink onto the bed, grab-bing the bracelet on my wrist like it might tether me to some-thing solid. But the string just digs into my skin. Tight. Meaningless. Just another lie.

My throat tightens, but I don't cry. I just sit there and let it sink in.

Everything they ever did. Every smile, every touch, every soft moment, all of it was paid for. None of it was real. They were here because Stevie paid them, because it was their job.

I just made it harder. I made them think I needed more, and they gave it to me because they had no other choice.

I stare at the floor, wishing it would just open up and swallow me whole. This is my fault. I ruined everything.

I squeeze my eyes shut and for a second, it feels like I'm back in the nightmare. Only this time, it's one I can't wake up from.

TWENTY-EIGHT

ROME

My voice keeps going. Flat. Controlled. Like I'm giving a damn press conference.

"We're just trying to look out for her." I say, shaking my head.

I'm downplaying it, and every person in this room knows it. But no one calls me out on it. Not Dallas. Not Niko. And definitely not Atlas, who's standing in the corner with his arms crossed, looking like he's watching a slow-motion train wreck.

"She needs protection. Not... whatever this is." Stevie waves her hand between the three of us. "And if you can't give her that without complicating it, then maybe she shouldn't be here."

Dallas rubs a hand down his face. Niko exhales through his nose. I clench my jaw.

"We get that you're concerned, but Violet is her own person with her own feelings. You can't expect us to just avoid her."

Stevie glares at me.

"You're being paid to keep her safe." She hisses. "Not to get attached."

The silence that follows feels like a closing door. Thick. Final. None of us say anything to dispute it. We can't. After Violet's attack, Stevie needed her somewhere safe, but she knew she'd never agree to be sequestered away with body-guards. The Reapers pitched the idea. They would propose the idea of her going into hiding, and the three of us would offer her a place to stay instead.

Dallas hated the plan from the start. He didn't want to lie to her. Niko and I weren't thrilled either, until they threw in an exclusivity contract. If we agreed, all our jobs from here on out would be for them. No more chasing random clients, no more splitting focus. With the added cash incentive, it was too good of an offer to pass up. So we took it, and I didn't think about the consequences.

Seems like I've been doing that a lot lately.

I let her kiss me. I let her crawl into my bed. I let myself fall for her. And now I'm forcing myself to downplay it because that's easier than telling them the truth. That I lost control. That I'd do it again. That I don't regret a goddamn second of it.

Then I hear it. Not the silence. Not the breathing. Some-thing else. *Ollie's paws.* Light. Quick. Fading. I go still. I know that sound. I've heard it every morning since she moved in, and it only means one thing.

She's awake.

I push off the wall and start for the hallway.

Stevie's voice cuts in behind me. "Where are you going?"

I don't answer, because if I stop, I might not go at all. I just move. Fast and focused, like I already know what I'm about to find.

The hallway's empty when I step out. I round the corner just in time to see her bedroom door shut. *Softly.* Almost like she didn't want anyone to hear it.

I stop in front of her door and press my hand against the wood like maybe I'll feel something through it. Like I can sense her on the other side, reaching back. But there's nothing. No sound, no movement, nothing at all. I could knock. I could say something. I don't, because if she was listening; I don't have an excuse for what she heard. Not a good one, anyway.

So I go back to my room. Lie down in the bed that still smells like her. Pull the covers up and pretend I don't feel the cold spot where she used to be.

————

BY THE TIME I hear movement outside my door again, the sun's already up. Soft footsteps. Cabinet doors opening and closing. The clink of glass. *Violet*.

I get up, throw on a sweatshirt and joggers, and race out of my room to find her. When I step into the kitchen, I see her standing there cooking like nothing's wrong. She's got her lavender hair tied back, sleeves pushed up, and she's standing at the stove in a hoodie that's way too big on her with Ollie laying down at her feet. She doesn't flinch when she sees me.

"Morning," she says, like it's the most normal thing in the world. "Want breakfast?"

My eye twitches.

She sounds… off.

"Violet."

She glances over her shoulder, smile faint. "Hmm?"

"We should talk."

She turns back to the pan. "What about?"

"Last night."

She flips the eggs in the pan with no hesitation. "What about it?"

I take a step closer. "You left."

"Oh, I figured you had plans. Thought I'd give you space."

I watch her. She's too calm. Too even. Her voice is soft, but there's no warmth in it. Just… politeness and precision. Like she rehearsed every line.

"You don't have to pretend." I say.

"I'm not." She says, sliding the eggs onto a plate and setting it on the counter. "You should eat."

Then she brushes past me like nothing's changed. Like last night was just a favor, not a memory burned into my skin. Like we didn't spend the night pressed so close together I forgot where I ended and she began. She doesn't touch me, doesn't look back, doesn't pause.

I almost look at her wrist to check to see if she's still wearing it. But I don't, because I'm not sure I could handle it if she wasn't. I stare at the plate and my stomach turns. Not because of the food, but because I've seen this version of her before. The one that smiles through pain. The one that keeps everyone at a safe distance by making it look easy. That's not the girl I carried into my bed last night. That girl trusted me.

This one? This one's just going through the motions. And I don't know how to reach her anymore.

TWENTY-NINE

VIOLET

I wake up already knowing what I have to do. Not what I want. Not what I feel like.m Just… what's necessary.

Pretend nothing's changed. Pretend I didn't hear my sister spell it out in plain English. That they're being paid. That everything I thought might've been real was just obligation dressed up in affection.

I can't break again. I won't. It's embarrassing. It's exhausting. And it's useless. So I do what I've always done when the truth eats through my chest like acid. I shut it out, push it down, and lock it behind a careful smile.

That's the thing people don't tell you about trauma. Sometimes surviving it isn't about fighting. Sometimes it's about acting normal enough so that no one tries to look too closely. It's easier to hide the wreckage when no one suspects it's there.

I'm good at that. Too good, probably.

So I get up, tie my hair back, throw on a hoodie, and walk into the kitchen like it's just another morning. Because if they're going to treat me like a job, I can treat this like a routine.

I start cooking. Not because I'm hungry. I don't think I could stomach a bite if I tried. But cooking is easy. Mechanical. It gives me something to focus on besides the spiral in my chest.

If I'm doing something, anything, they won't look too hard. They won't see the girl who was stupid enough to believe any of this was real.

I'm flipping the second batch of pancakes when I hear hesitant footsteps approaching. *It's Rome.* He pauses in the doorway like he doesn't know if he should interrupt. I don't turn to look.

"Morning," I say, light and sweet. "Want breakfast?"

There's a pause. I can feel him staring, and I already know what's coming.

"Violet."

I glance over my shoulder, meet his eyes, and smile like it's a perfectly normal day. "Hmm?"

"We should talk."

I shrug and flip the eggs. "About?"

"Last night."

"What about it?" I ask, keeping my voice casual.

"You left," he says.

"Oh, I figured you had plans." I lie, turning off the stove. "Thought I'd give you space."

I slide a plate of eggs and bacon across the counter toward him.

"You don't have to pretend," he says.

"I'm not." I rinse the spatula and dry my hands, voice perfectly even. "You should eat."

Then I walk past him. I know he's still standing there, watching me, but I don't care. Or at least, I'm trying really hard not to.

Dallas walks in next, yawning as he grabs the mug I

already filled for him. He wraps an arm around my shoulder in that lazy way he always does, like he didn't betray me too.

"Damn, Darlin'," he says. "You didn't have to do all this."

"Didn't have anything better to do," I answer with a tight smile.

He doesn't notice.

Niko shows up a minute later, looking like he hasn't slept. His jaw is tight, his shoulders tense, and he doesn't say a word. He just heads to the coffeemaker and pours himself a cup.

Dallas sips his coffee. Rome pokes at the plate in front of him, barely eating. Niko stares at the floor.

I wipe the counter clean and listen to the silence that builds around us. Full of things no one wants to say. It almost feels normal. But it's not, because I know now... I'm not someone they chose. I'm someone they were paid to choose.

So I smile, I clean up, and I do what I should've done when I first got here... become the version of myself that's easiest to deal with. Because that's who they really wanted living in their home all along.

———

THE SECOND THE bedroom door shuts behind me, the smile drops and my shoulders fall. I stand there for a moment, pressing my forehead against the door. *God, I feel stupid.*

For every touch I mistook for something real. For every night I sat in this room wondering if maybe, just maybe, one of them was thinking about me too. For every second I thought I could build something out of borrowed time and forced proximity.

They were never mine. Not even close. I was just someone they were paid to protect. And God, I tried so hard to be worth keeping.

I shut my eyes for a second, but it doesn't help. Because

the ache isn't in my head, it's in my chest. Twisting sharp and slow. I wish it would carve out the part of me that still misses them.

I'm so tired of hurting. I've been carrying guilt for weeks, letting it rot inside me and fester, because I didn't want to be a burden. I didn't want to give them a reason to pull away and lose what I thought I had. But it turns out, I never had anything to begin with.

So what am I even protecting anymore?

I grab my phone from the nightstand and scroll through my contacts until I land on her name. *Stevie.* I hit the call button, and she answers on the second ring.

"Alex?" She says, her voice sounding a little groggy. "Is everything okay?"

I don't ease into it or soften the edges.

"I've been getting threatening texts," I say flatly.

There's a pause. "From who?"

"Unknown number," I say. "Nothing direct. But it's him. The man who bought me."

"How do you know?"

I stare ahead, voice steady. "Because he said he'd come back for me. And now he has. I think he hired my attacker, too."

I hear the air rush out of her lungs. "Jesus, Alex. When did this start?"

"A few weeks after I moved into the apartment."

"What the hell, Alex? Why didn't you tell me?"

"Because I didn't want to make things worse." I swallow. "I didn't want to be your problem again."

"Alex-"

"It's fine."

"No, it's not. You're not a problem."

It's a lie. A sweet one at that.

"Did you tell the guys?" She asks.

"No."

There's a heavy pause. "Okay. I'll get Tristan on this. We'll track it, and we'll loop the guys in-"

"You don't have to do all that."

"I do. You're not safe."

"I know."

"Then why are you acting like this doesn't matter?"

"Because it doesn't change anything. Nothing is going to stop him."

"Alex, please just let me-"

"I'll forward the messages." I pause, the silence stretching like a held breath. "I just thought you'd want to know. Since you're still paying them for the illusion of my safety."

Then I hang up. And the quiet that follows feels like the truest thing I've heard all day.

THIRTY

DALLAS

I TOLD MYSELF I'D LEAVE HER ALONE. THAT IT WAS BETTER TO give her space. But here I am, knocking on her door anyway.

Her room is quiet when I enter, lit by soft light pouring in through the window. She's curled up in the corner of her bed, legs tucked beneath her, a book resting open in her lap. One of my hoodies hangs off her shoulders, sleeves bunched at her wrists, and her long lavender hair is tied up in a lazy knot plopped on the top of her head.

Ollie lifts his head from the floor and blinks at me with that calm, knowing gaze. He doesn't trot towards me, like he normally does. He just lies there, silently judging me from his spot at her feet.

"Hey Stranger," I say.

She doesn't look up. "You knock now? That's new."

"Trying to be polite," I answer, stepping further in. "Didn't know if you were busy."

She doesn't tell me to leave, but she doesn't invite me to stay either. So I move to the edge of the bed and sit, careful not to jostle her space. The mattress dips under my weight, but she doesn't acknowledge it, just flips a page like I'm not even here.

"You okay?"

"Yeah. Of course." Her reply is too fast, too smooth.

Her fingers tighten around the book's spine, and she releases a gentle sigh. I lean forward, elbows on my knees, trying to figure out a way to reach her. "Hey, so I was thinking. You know that weirdly sad movie we watched last week? The one about the pop stars who fight demons?"

Her lips twitch. *Almost.* "That isn't a sad movie, Dallas."

I grin. "You cried."

She glances at me. "So did you."

There it is. A flicker of the girl I know. The one I've missed like hell for the last couple of days.

My heart thuds like it's happy to get a glimpse of her too.

"Anyway, I was wondering if you wanted to do a rewatch with me?"

V shakes her head without looking at me. "Not now, maybe later."

I shift closer, reach out, and brush my fingers against her knee. Her gaze drops to the spot where my skin touches hers, but she doesn't move.

"Where are you?" I murmur.

She stiffens. "I'm right here."

I give her a sad smile. "No, you're not."

The silence that follows feels like it's pressing against my ribs. I move my hand up to gently cup the side of her face. She meets my eyes, and for one second, she leans into my touch.

I inch towards her. Close enough to smell the faint scent of vanilla clinging to her skin. Close enough to remember how her lips felt against mine the night I almost lost Ollie. Desperate, warm, and real. Like she needed me just as much as I needed her. My chest aches with the memory.

I swallow and lean in for a kiss. But when I'm a breath

away, she turns her head and my lips graze her cheek instead. It's not a full-blown rejection, but it sure as hell feels like it.

She pulls away and smiles like she didn't just rip my soul out. "I should finish this chapter."

Ollie lifts his head slightly, ears twitching. Watching me like he knows I just lost something.

I lean back and don't say anything. Because what's there to say? I don't need her to kiss me. I don't even need her to want me back. I just need *her*. And despite her being right here, smiling at me like everything's fine, I can't shake the feeling that she's already gone.

I shut her door behind me quietly and I rub a hand over my face. *What the fuck was I thinking?* I knew something was off with her, knew something was wrong the minute she gave me that fake smile in the kitchen a few days ago. And instead of slowing down, asking, and listening. I did what I always do. Tried to fix it with charm. With touch. With heat. Used *that* instead of my words.

Because deep down, I still think that's all I'm good for. A distraction. Something easy and shallow. Something that feels like comfort even when it's not.

I thought maybe if I could make her feel wanted, it would help, but all I did was make her pull away. And that smile she gave me before I left… that wasn't relief. It was resignation. The kind people wear when they're tired of pretending everything's okay. I thought I was fixing shit between us, but I think I just made it worse.

———

I PACE DOWN THE HALL, not really thinking about where I'm going until I hit the elevator. I need to move. Do something. Let my body burn so my head can shut up for a while.

I make it to the gym and push the door open. The place is

empty, but the lights are on, and the scent of rubber mats, steel plates, and disinfectant clings in the air.

I toss my hoodie on the bench and grab the nearest barbell, rolling my shoulders back like that'll shake off the ache crawling under my skin. I don't warm up. I don't stretch. I load the bar, lie back, and press until my arms are screaming. Until the regret in my chest gets drowned out by something physical.

The door opens halfway through my third set.

Niko walks in, shirtless, silent, rolling his neck like he has a lifetime of tension in his shoulders. He doesn't say anything, just nods at me once and starts setting up at the cable machine.

A minute later, Rome slips in too. He heads for the treadmill without a word, pulls his hood up, and starts running.

I drop the bar with a sharp exhale, sit up, and wipe my hands on my shorts.

"She's not talking to me anymore," Niko mutters finally.

I grab a towel and pat my brow. "Same."

He exhales through his nose. "She won't even look me in the eye."

"She does with me," I say. "But it's not the same."

Niko grunts. "She smile at you?"

I hesitate. "Yeah. But not the genuine kind. It's polite, like she's trying to prove she's fine."

"But she's not," he says.

"No. She isn't."

Niko paces a bit, dragging a hand through his hair. "She was opening up again. I could feel it. And now? Nothing."

"Something changed," I say. "I just don't know what."

"You think something happened with Stevie?"

I'm about to answer when the treadmill slows down behind us. Rome hops off and pulls back his hood. "She was awake that night."

Niko and I both turn.

"What?" I ask.

Rome keeps his voice flat. "The night Stevie came by. I didn't see her, but I know she was awake."

Niko narrows his eyes. "How?"

Rome exhales slowly. "Because when I left, she was in my bed, and when I came back, she was gone."

The silence is instant.

Niko's arms fall to his sides, his brow pinched. Not angry, just processing.

My hand tightens around the edge of the bench.

"She stayed with you that night?" I ask, quieter than I mean to.

Rome nods once and swallows hard.

There's no tension. No ego. Just the quiet ache of us all realizing we're not the only ones she matters to.

After a beat, Niko looks at him. "So you think she heard us."

"I think she heard something," Rome says. "Maybe not the whole thing, but enough."

I nod my head. "If she thinks we were only ever here for her because we were hired... then yeah. Of course she's shutting down."

No one says anything, because there's nothing left to say. She let us in, and we gave her every fucking reason to regret it.

THIRTY-ONE

VIOLET

THE WATER IS TOO HOT. I SCRUB AT THE SAME PLATE FOR THE third time, letting the heat bite into my skin until my fingertips sting. The soap suds slide over porcelain and disappear down the drain in lazy spirals.

It's mindless. Soothing in a way. Something to do with my hands so the focus isn't on the ache still tucked beneath my ribs. The apartment phone rings, sharp and sudden, cutting through the quiet like a blade. I dry my hands on a dish towel and cross the kitchen to answer it.

"Hello?"

"Miss Warner?" a voice says through the speaker. "You've got a delivery downstairs."

I blink. "I didn't order anything."

"It's addressed to you."

I pause.

"Okay," I say, too confused to say anything else. "I'll be right down."

The moment I step into the lobby, I see it. A massive bouquet of roses. At least three dozen, maybe more. Deep red,

Dramatic. Wrapped in expensive paper with gold ribbon curling down the sides. They're sitting on a rolling cart beside the desk, looking completely out of place next to the matte concrete walls and polished steel security posts.

The front desk attendant smiles politely. "These came for you."

I walk over slowly, like the flowers might bite. The scent is immediate. Overpowering, syrupy, invasive. I force my expression to stay neutral as I scribble my name on the tablet and accept the bouquet.

"They're beautiful," the guard offers.

I nod, but I don't agree. I hate roses. They're showy and impersonal. A lazy default when someone wants to look thoughtful without trying. And the moment I lift them into my arms, the weight of that truth hits hard. One of the guys bought me roses.

They probably meant well, but it just proves what I've been worried about all along. They don't really know me, not in the way I want them to.

The elevator ride back up is quiet. The roses feel like they're expanding with every floor, taking up more space in my arms, more air in my lungs.

When I make it to our floor, I set the bouquet on the kitchen island, and stare at it for far too long.

———

AN HOUR LATER, I'm curled up on the couch when I hear the elevator ding. Dallas strolls in first, his hands full of dog treats, with Ollie trotting by his side. Rome and Niko follow behind him, both dressed down in plain tees and joggers, mid-conversation about something I don't quite catch. They all stop short when they see the bouquet on the counter.

"Who are those from?" Rome asks, shifting his weight like he's bracing for an answer he won't like.

I force a small smile. "There's no note. You tell me."

Dallas shakes his head. "Wasn't me. I would've picked violets. Obviously."

Niko frowns. "We all know you hate the smell of roses."

I blink. "Wait. None of you sent them?"

They all shake their heads in unison.

A chill creeps across my skin, blooming at the base of my neck and crawling down my arms. *They* didn't send them. None of them did.

I stare at the roses. The petals seem sharper now, too red. Too *perfect*. A sick feeling pools in my gut. My heart thumps hard against my ribs, faster now, like it already knows something I don't.

I take a step back. Then another. My breath quickens. I don't want to look. I don't want to *know*, but my hands move anyway, numb and shaky as I reach for my phone on the counter.

My thumb unlocks the screen. And there it is... a new message from an unknown number.

Enjoy the roses. They're perfect.
Just like you.

The phone slips from my hand and hits the hardwood with a dull thud. The noise makes all three of the guys look at me, but I can't speak. My heart stutters and then takes off, pounding so fast it feels like it might break free from my chest. The edges of the room go blurry. The air feels thick. Heavy. Unbreathable. Because it's *him*.

He knows. Where I breathe. Where I sleep. Where I thought I was safe. The color drains from my face as my eyes lock on the flowers like they might open their petals and swallow me whole.

Rome says my name and a question, I think. But I don't answer. Because the words are stuck somewhere in the back of my throat, blocked by panic and disbelief and fear so loud it drowns out everything else.

Not here. Not where I thought I was finally safe. I press my back into the couch, curling into myself as the weight of it all crashes down. He found me. He fucking found me.

THIRTY-TWO

NIKO

THE SOUND OF HER PHONE HITTING THE FLOOR SHOULDN'T MAKE my heart stop, but it does. I hear it before I see it. That soft clatter of glass against wood, sharp enough to cut through the conversation like a blade. I turn just in time to see the color drain from her face. Eyes wide, chest rising like she's drowning in open air.

"Violet?" Rome says her name first.

She doesn't answer. Her hands tremble, and she curls in on herself, like the weight of something invisible just crushed down on her. Something's wrong. It's written all over her face.

I step closer and reach for the phone she dropped. The screen's still on with a message opened.

Enjoy the roses. They're perfect. Just like you.

My stomach turns to ice.

"Rome," I snap, tossing the phone at him. "Call security. Now."

He's already moving, fishing his phone from his pocket and heading toward the office.

Dallas is crouched next to Violet in seconds, hands out, voice soft but shaking. "It's okay, Darlin'. You're okay. You're safe."

Ollie nuzzles her hand. She doesn't respond. Her breathing's gone ragged. Her shoulders shake, like she's trying to pull herself inward and disappear.

I step closer, crouch low in front of her, careful not to touch her. "Vi," I say, quiet and measured. Hoping my voice might anchor her if I find the right tone. "Can you look at me?"

She doesn't. She's somewhere else. Somewhere far away, and I know exactly where. I've seen that look before, in her eyes, in mine.

Dallas reaches for her hand. She jerks away like he burned her. *Fuck.* He pulls back instantly, eyes wide with guilt.

"She's panicking," I whisper. "It's a trauma response. This isn't just a scare."

Dallas sits back on his heels, helpless, like the breath's been punched out of him. "I didn't know. I didn't-"

"It's not your fault," I cut in, sharper than I mean to. "She has no control over her reactions right now."

Violet lets out a sound. It's small, broken, almost a sob, but it dies in her throat before it fully escapes her. I can't take it anymore.

I move in slowly, sinking onto the floor beside her, not touching, just near enough that she can feel me if she needs to.

"I'm right here," I whisper. "We all are. He doesn't get to have you. Not here. Not anymore."

Her lips part like she wants to say something, but nothing

comes out. Dallas drops his head into his hands. Rome walks back into the room, his expression cold and controlled, but I see the cracks behind his eyes.

"Bobby's contacting the flower company that sent them," he says. "I told him to cross-reference every name and face from the delivery log today."

"Good," I bite out.

"We should sweep the security feeds too." Dallas says, swallowing. "Just in case he's lingering around."

"I'm on it," Rome says.

Violet curls tighter into herself, her cheek pressed to the seat of the couch, arms wrapped around her knees. She's silent. But her breathing hasn't evened out.

I glance at the kitchen island. The roses are still there. Red. Blooming. Fucking mocking all of us.

"Let's get these the hell out of here." I say, standing abruptly.

"No," Dallas says, looking up. "We should bag them. If they were brought in by him, there could be fingerprints."

He's right. I grab a pair of gloves from the utility drawer and carefully gather the bouquet, not caring if I crush a few petals. I stuff them into a trash bag, tie it, and toss it on the balcony.

When I walk back in, Dallas is still sitting next to her, and Rome's on the phone again, pacing. Violet hasn't moved, but her eyes are open.

A hollow ache opens in my chest. I've seen that look before, and I know how it ends if someone doesn't step in.

"She needs Stevie," I say, looking to Rome.

He stops pacing and nods once. "I'll call her."

"I'll stay with her," Dallas says, voice rough.

Rome turns toward the door. I crouch again beside her, slower this time. Her eyes flick toward me, barely a glance, but it's something.

"You're safe," I whisper, barely more than breath. "You're safe."

Her fingers twitch, and for the first time since the panic hit, she blinks like she's coming back to herself.

I don't say anything else. I just stay there. Close. Solid. Because right now, she doesn't need saving. She just needs to know she's not alone.

THIRTY-THREE

STEVIE

I don't ask questions when Rome calls. He says six words: *She needs you. It's bad. Hurry*, and that's enough to make my heart claw at my ribs.

Tris is already grabbing his keys before I hang up. Ezra, Atlas, and Cyrus follow with no need for explanation. No one says it, but we all feel it. Something's wrong with Alex. And whatever it is, we're not letting her face it alone.

By the time we make it to the penthouse, I'm already rehearsing worst-case scenarios in my head. Broken bones. Blood. Maybe a body. What I'm not prepared for is the silence.

When the elevator doors open, no one's shouting, no one's crying, but something is still very, very wrong. Alex is curled up on the couch, spine pressed to the corner like she's trying to sink into the cushions. Her hair's a mess, her face pale, and her eyes... *fuck*, her eyes are blank.

Dallas is a few feet away, sitting on the floor like the weight of it has crushed him. His puppy is next to him, looking even sadder than he does. Rome's by the window, pacing like he wants to punch something. Niko's perched on the edge of the coffee table, elbows on his knees, watching her like she might vanish if he blinks.

Atlas stiffens beside me. His hand clenches into a fist at his side, like he's holding back the urge to storm over and fix it all with brute force.

Ezra's jaw ticks once, twice. His entire body goes still, but I know him well enough to see the way he catalogues every detail. Every breath, every tremble, as if memorizing them will somehow make her okay.

Cyrus is the first to move. Quiet. Controlled. He steps around the couch and grabs the throw blanket from the armrest, and gently tucks it around Alex's shoulders with the kind of tenderness you wouldn't expect from a man who's killed for less.

Tristan flicks his gaze toward Alex and his jaw tightens. He pulls his phone out, tapping commands with mechanical precision, no doubt already hacking into the building's security feed.

I move toward her slowly, careful not to spook her.

"Alex," I say.

Nothing. Not a twitch. Not a blink. I crouch beside her and place a hand on the couch cushion, close enough for her to feel me, far enough not to trigger whatever the hell's holding her hostage.

"I'm here, baby sis," I murmur. "I've got you."

She doesn't look at me, but something shifts in her eyes. Her breath catches in her throat. Her jaw ticks and she swallows like she's trying not to cry, and then she breaks. Silently. Tears spill down her cheeks, no sound, no warning, they just fall with quiet devastation.

I climb onto the couch and wrap my arms around her, tucking her into me like I used to when she was five and afraid of thunderstorms. She folds into my chest like muscle memory, like she never forgot how to let me hold her, even though it's been years since I last did it.

"I'm sorry I didn't tell you sooner," she whispers, voice hoarse. "I just didn't want to burden you again."

My chest clenches as I squeeze her tighter. "You were never a burden to me, Al. You've always been my lifeline."

Alex swallows and blinks like she's trying to digest my words.

"He sent flowers," she says, broken. "He knows where I am."

I go still. And I'm suddenly fighting the urge to rip someone's spine out with my bare hands.

"Are you sure they're from him?"

She nods, her forehead still pressed to my collarbone. "He sent a text. He wanted me to know he sent them."

I clench my jaw so hard it hurts. *Motherfucker.* I look up at the guys. Their faces say everything I'm thinking. Dallas looks wrecked. Rome's gone stone-cold. And Niko's already gone somewhere dark, like a switch has been flipped inside of him.

Good. Let it flip. Because if this bastard thinks he can crawl out of whatever hole he's been rotting in and come for her again, he's about to learn what it feels like to be hunted.

I turn back to Alex. She's gripping the front of my leather jacket so hard her fingers are turning white.

"We've got you," I say, threading my fingers through her hair. "You're safe."

"It doesn't feel like it," she croaks.

I press a kiss to the top of her head, my throat tight. "That's because he's playing mind games, but he messed up by leaving a trail."

Her fingers twitch. "I didn't mean for this to happen. I thought if I just ignored it, it would go away."

"It's not your fault." I whisper. "You had to be so brave and so strong for so long now. Of course you tried to handle it on your own. But we're here now…" I pause, looking around the room, "and we've all got you."

Her body sags against mine and I tug her even closer. She doesn't have to face him alone anymore. That's what we're here for. And if that sick bastard really is back? If he's watching her and planning something? Then he just made the biggest mistake of his life.

THIRTY-FOUR

ROME

THE WALK TO OUR SECURITY ROOM IS SHORT. TRISTAN'S ALREADY there when I arrive. The monitors in front of him cycle between feeds. Exterior, lobby, elevator, garage. I step inside and shut the door behind me.

"What do we have?" I ask.

"Traffic cams caught a black SUV idling near the east entrance the night Stevie and Atlas visited," Tristan says without looking up. "No plates. No identifying marks."

My spine locks.

"When?"

He taps a few keys and pulls the feed up on the largest monitor.

"Here."

The timestamp flashes.

1:27 AM. Five days ago.

The same night. The same fucking night she was in my bed, dusted in sugar and smiling like the world was finally quiet.

I step closer to the screen. The SUV's windows are blacked

out. No decals. No movement. But it's there. Sitting across the street, engine on, lights off. Watching. Waiting.

Stevie and Atlas left around 2:00 A.M. I remember it now. I didn't check the cameras after I went back to my room. I didn't think I needed to.

"Zoom in," I say.

Tristan does. The image is grainy, there's still no plate, but the silhouette of the driver is visible. Big frame, white shirt, with a dark coat slung over the seat. I stare at the screen in disbelief.

"How long was he parked there?"

"Thirty-seven minutes," Tristan replies. "He never got out of the car and drove off just before 2:04 A.M."

I scrub a hand down my face. He didn't need to get out of the car because he wasn't here for Stevie. He was here for *her*. I should've noticed he followed them here, but I didn't. She was in my bed. Exposed and unprotected.

I steady myself on the desk. "Any chance he came back later?"

"Working on the scans now."

I nod once and back away from the monitor, hoping the distance might help me breathe easier. It doesn't. She's been in danger the whole time, and I was too fucking busy falling for her to notice.

———

I LOOK in the mirror and can't stand the reflection staring back at me. He's pompous. *Fucking arrogant.* Thinks he's got it all under control, when in reality, he hasn't been controlling anything.

My fist snaps forward before I can stop it. Glass shatters under my knuckles, sending shards raining into the sink. The pain doesn't bother me. Neither does the blood. I've seen worse. Inflicted worse.

I flex my hand under the stream and watch the water run pink. It's not enough to feel like penance, but it'll have to do.

Violet is in danger, and that's on *me*. I was supposed to protect her, keep her out of harm's way. Instead, I was in bed with her with my head full of sugar and skin and her soft breaths.

I didn't just let my guard down. I fucking dismantled it. And now she's curled on the couch like something's been carved out of her. Crying in silence while the man who broke her sends flowers to my fucking home like it's a game to him.

I turn off the faucet, grab a roll of gauze, and wind it tight around my hand. Blood seeps through almost immediately, so I add a few more layers until the red disappears.

When it's covered, I flex my fingers, swallow the ache, and step out of the bathroom like nothing's wrong.

The living room is quiet when we come back.

Violet is still huddled in the corner of the couch with Ollie at her feet. Stevie's on the couch beside her with one arm curled around her. Atlas and Cyrus are half-asleep in the armchairs. Niko is leaning against the wall with his arms crossed. Dallas is on the floor with Ezra sitting next to him mumbling something about Ollie chewing his shoelaces. And Tristan is posted up by the window, keeping watch.

They didn't leave. None of them did. *Good.* Violet needs all of us right now. Even if she won't say so.

I stand in the doorway for a long moment, just watching her. She isn't crying anymore, but she's not really present either. Her fingers are twisted in the blanket, and her eyes fixed on the edge of the coffee table like it might bite her if she looks away too long.

She's freezing. I can tell by the way her shoulders bunch under the throw. So, I head for the linen closet. When I come back, I've got the thickest comforter we own. Soft, worn, and still faintly smelling like the dryer sheet she always sneaks into the laundry.

I walk over without a word. She doesn't look at me, just keeps staring at the table like she's underwater and everything's muffled. I crouch beside her and unfold the comforter slowly, careful not to make her flinch. Then I tuck it around her. Wrapping it gently around her shoulders, and making sure her hands are covered too, because they always get cold first. I know that about her. I know *a lot* of things I probably shouldn't about her.

When I finish, I rest my hand on the edge of the couch, just for a second, to show that I'm here for her, and that I'll always will be. Her eyes flick to me, barely, but it's enough for me to know she got the message. I pull back and settle on the floor next to her. When I glance up, Stevie's watching me.

She says nothing, just studies my face like she's trying to fit something together.Then she shifts, tugs Violet just a little closer, and mouths- *Thank you.*

THIRTY-FIVE

VIOLET

The world comes back to me in pieces. The weight of Stevie's arm around me. The people in the room, surrounding me. The quiet murmur of words I can't make out. And then I sense *Rome* step into the room.

The air shifts as he moves towards me, and his footsteps soften the closer he gets, like he's afraid he'll spook me. I feel the brush of fabric first, then the weight of a comforter settling over my shoulders.

He doesn't speak or touch more than he has to, but I *know* it's him. He moves like someone who's memorized every part of me.

I don't look at him. I can't. Everything in me feels raw, like my skin's been peeled back and all of my nerves are now exposed. But in my head, something cracks open, and now I can't stop thinking about him.

———

IT'S MORNING, I think. The lamp is still on, but the light through the windows is different. Pale and soft, like the city hasn't decided if it wants to wake up yet.

Everyone's still here. Stevie's beside me, her arm heavy and warm where it wraps around my back. Her fingers twitch slightly in her sleep, like she's dreaming. Rome's still on the floor, his head tipped back against the couch, with his eyes closed and one hand resting near the hem of the comforter. Ezra's sleeping on the other side of the coffee table. Dallas is curled on the floor with Ollie half-draped over his legs. Niko is posted against the wall, observing everything. Atlas and Cyrus are knocked out in the armchairs. And Tristan is at the kitchen table tapping on his phone silently.

No one left. Not when I broke, not when I stopped speaking, not even when I couldn't look at them. *They all stayed.*

I blink hard, staring at the seams of the blanket between my fingers. This is the weakest I've ever been. The most exposed, the most humiliated, the most *honest,* and it's also the most love I've ever felt.

Not just from Stevie and The Reapers. But from *them.* The men I swore were just doing a job. The ones I told myself didn't actually care. Rome didn't have to kneel beside me and cover me in warmth like I was something precious. But he did. Dallas didn't have to sit on the floor like my pain had knocked him over too. But he did. And Niko didn't have to stay with me when he's never been the kind to sit still. But he did.

My throat tightens. If this is what love looks like, quiet and steady and unexpected and *real*, then maybe I've been wrong about what I deserve all along. Maybe I'm not a burden. Maybe I'm just… loved.

———

I AWAKE AGAIN SOMETIME LATER from noise in the kitchen. I hear a low curse, the clang of a pan, and something sizzling a little too loud to be intentional. I sit up slightly, careful not to jostle Stevie, and peek over the back of the couch.

Dallas is standing in front of the stove with a spatula in one hand and a dish towel in the other, looking like he's preparing for war. His hair is a mess, his T-shirt is wrinkled, and his eyes are still puffy from sleep. But, he's trying and it's endearing as hell. He tosses something in the pan and immediately recoils when smoke billows upward.

I watch him fan it with the towel like that'll help, muttering under his breath. Rome walks past the hallway and pauses, blinking once at the chaos before continuing on. The corner of my mouth lifts. Dallas flips what looks to be a very sad attempt at a pancake and glares at the pan like it betrayed him when he sees the charred surface.

"I can help," I say, my voice hoarse.

Everyone looks up.

Dallas turns, blinking like he's not sure he heard me right. "You... want to?"

"I think I need to," I murmur, pushing the blanket off of my legs. "Before you burn the whole place down."

He steps aside immediately, handing me the spatula like it's sacred. I roll up the sleeves of my sweatshirt and grab a clean pan.

The kitchen smells like sugar and burnt batter and something else I can't quite name. Home, maybe.

Rome appears again, this time with a mug in his hand. He sets it quietly on the counter beside me. I glance down. It's my favorite tea. He doesn't say a word, just walks away. I keep cooking.

Dallas sticks by me, watching me like he might learn something, even though we both know he won't. By the time I plate everything, eggs, toast, actual pancakes that aren't charcoal, everyone else has stirred.

Ezra claims the first plate with a low whistle. Tristan mumbles something about "finally edible," and Niko gives me the closest thing to a smile I've ever seen on his face.

They're eating *my* food. And for the first time since those flowers showed up, I feel like I can breathe again. Not because everything's fixed, not because I'm healed, but because they're still here. And maybe that's all I've ever needed.

THIRTY-SIX

VIOLET

I DON'T FEEL IT RIGHT AWAY. THE SHIFT, THE PULL, THE WARNING. I'm in the kitchen rinsing dishes, humming something under my breath, when my phone buzzes.

A single vibration against the kitchen counter. I dry my hands and pick it up. There's no preview. Just a message icon with a small gray dot. I open it. And the world stops.

It's a photo. Of the living room. Of all of them. *Sleeping.*

Stevie's lying beside me. Dallas is on the floor. Niko is nodding off against the wall. Ollie is tucked under Ezra's leg. Rome's back is against the couch, like he didn't mean to fall asleep. Tris is slumped over at the kitchen island, and Cyrus and Atlas are slouched in their chairs like they're still on alert, even while they're sleeping.

All of them. The photo was taken from the balcony. My stomach lurches.

Another buzz. A second message.

> Come meet me alone. Or they're all dead.

And below it is a location pin.

I click the link and see it's a warehouse downtown in the abandoned district in Caspian Valley. I know the area; I know the danger, but I also know he's not bluffing.

My fingers go cold. The buzzing in my ears starts again, louder this time. I glance back into the living room. Stevie's laughing at something Ezra said. Dallas is licking syrup from his fingers. Ollie's begging for scraps.

They're all *right here*. Safe. Happy. Whole. And they have no idea how much danger they're in *because of me.* I was selfish enough to believe I could have this. That I could escape his clutches and live a normal life. And now he's going to rip it all away. Unless I do something to stop him.

I pocket the phone and slip out of the kitchen quietly. The laughter from the living room fades as I move down the hall. Every step feels like it echoes louder than the last.

I slip into Rome's room. It smells like him. Sharp, clean, cedar and something darker I've never been able to name. His bed is perfectly made, and his closet door is cracked just enough to show a row of black shirts lined up like soldiers.

I head to the dresser and tug the bottom drawer open. The hidden case clicks open. The gun is heavy. Cold. Familiar in a way that makes my stomach turn. *It's the same kind as Atlas'.*

I check the magazine, like I've seen the guys do hundreds of times, pop it back in, and thumb the safety. Then I slip it into the waistband of my sweats, tug the hem of my hoodie down to cover it, and press the drawer shut. Rome won't notice it's gone. He has his own arsenal in their artillery room.

I step back, glance around to make sure everything is how

I found it, and pause in the doorway. I don't know how this ends. But I know what I have to do now.

THIRTY-SEVEN

VIOLET

The second I step through the warehouse doors, I know I'm being watched. It's in the air. The weight of it. The silence that isn't really silence. It's the kind that rings in your ears and dares you to move.

The door slams shut behind me. *Hard.* I don't flinch, but my fingers twitch at my sides. The air is thick with dust and the metallic stench of rusting steel. Moonlight filters through cracks in the roof, casting silver lines across the concrete floor like the whole building's been cut open.

Every step echoes. Louder than the last. My sneakers scuff against the floor as I move deeper, past abandoned machinery and skeletal rafters looming like predators overhead. The only sound is the steady, pounding rhythm in my chest.

I keep walking. Even when it feels like something's crawling up the back of my neck. Even when I swear I hear a breath that isn't mine. Then I see it. A single beam of light. Artificial and cutting through the dark like a spotlight. Standing dead center in its path is *him*, looking like he's been waiting centuries for me to arrive.

His hands are in his pockets. His head tilted slightly. His smile, *God*. That smile always made my skin crawl and it still does.

"My perfect girl," he croons, his voice low and whiney. "You came."

He moves forward a step. "How brave of you." Another step. "How stupid of you."

His eyes trail down my frame, over my blank expression, past my oversized sweatsuit, and down to the sneakers on my feet. His smile widens like I've just proven some sick theory right.

"Come here," he says, holding out a hand like I might actually take it.

I don't move.

He sighs as if I've disappointed him. "Always so difficult."

Then he closes the space himself. Each step is slow and measured. The way someone might approach a deer in the wild.

He stops inches in front of me. And then he leans in and licks me, from the curve of my jaw to the temple of my forehead.

I don't react, not on the outside. But inside? Everything screams.

I reach for the gun in my waistband, fingers wrapping tight around the grip as I raise it between us.

His hand snaps out, catches my wrist, squeezes hard enough to make my bones grind. He looks down, expression amused, curious even, until his eyes land on the tattoo peeking out of the top of my sweatpants.

It's the celestial moth I got with Niko, the one that erased his ugly mark for good. His smile drops. He pries the gun from my hand and shoves me to the ground as his expression twists into something feral.

"You think *this* makes you strong?" he sneers as he raises

my gun in the air. "You think covering my claim on you will change anything?"

I stare at him and say nothing.

He paces once in a tight circle, one hand dragging through his thinning blonde hair as he glares at me like I've offended him on a cosmic level.

"You are mine!" He snaps. "I'm the only one who's ever really seen you. The only one who's ever cared. And this, this is how you repay me?"

I laugh at his outburst. It bubbles up from somewhere deep, sounding hysterical and borderline unhinged.

He startles, and his mouth parts as if he doesn't know what to make of it. "What the fuck is wrong with you?"

I tilt my head and level him with a vicious glare. "I was just laughing at the irony."

"Of what?" He hisses.

I chance a glance over my shoulder. "Of them."

His eyes narrow as he searches the darkness, then *they* step out of the shadows.

Stevie, Dallas, Rome, Niko, Atlas, Ezra, Tristan, and Cyrus are all here. Ollie is too, crouched low with his hackles raised like he's waiting for the command.

All of their guns are raised. All of their expressions are fierce. All of their eyes are laser-focused on him.

My monster freezes and, in that moment, I see him for who he truly is. A pathetic, desperate, little man. He fumbles for the gun in his hand, *Rome's gun*, and spins it toward me with his finger on the trigger.

Click.

Nothing happens. There aren't any bullets in the chamber. I made sure of that on the drive over.

He pulls the trigger again, and again, staring at the gun in his hand in disbelief. His eyes snap to me, and they widen in disbelief.

I smile at him as I settle in line with everyone I've ever cared about. "You're so fucked."

THIRTY-EIGHT

DALLAS

I HATE SILENCE. I USED TO FIND COMFORT IN IT. BUT RIGHT NOW, it just reminds me of everything we lost.

Her voice. Her laughter. Her joy. He took all that from her. Tortured her for months right under our fucking noses. So no, I don't want silence.

I want chaos. I want noise. I want his screams to drown out my memory of ever hearing hers.

Ezra's basement isn't like the rest of their bar. It's colder. Quieter. Like even the air down here knows something wicked's about to happen.

It's just the six of us down here. Me, Rome, Niko, Ezra, Cyrus, and Tristan. All of us gathered for one reason. To break the monster who broke her. The one who bought her, branded her, and raped her like the vile bastard he is.

He's escaped justice for long enough. But tonight? Tonight he's ours.

———

THE SECOND I SEE HIM, stripped down and chained up in the center of the basement like some mangy animal, something feral shifts in my chest. He's not as smug as he was when we dragged him in earlier. His blonde hair is matted to his forehead, his lips are split from Cyrus' earlier introduction, and there's a wild, darting panic in his eyes now.

Good. He should be scared. He should be terrified. Because what's coming for him is made of fucking nightmares.

Ezra grabs a pair of gloves off the tray and tosses them to me. "You ready?"

I pull them on without hesitation.

"No music?" Tristan quips from the corner, checking the calibration on one of the tools like he's tuning an instrument and not preparing for a bloodbath.

"I want to hear every second," I mutter, grabbing a wrench off the wall.

The motherfucker starts to shake.

"You don't understand," he rasps, voice fraying. "Whatever she told you. She's confused. She-"

I drive the wrench into his left kneecap. He screams. Loud. Messy. Pathetic.

"I understand enough," I say calmly, rotating my wrist like I'm checking the follow-through on a golf swing. "I understand you kept her locked up like an animal. I understand you made her bleed. And I understand you made her think she deserved it."

Another hit. *Crack.* His leg folds wrong, and Cyrus lets out a low whistle.

"Dallas is usually the sweet one," he says to no one in particular, "but damn if he doesn't turn savage when you fuck with someone he loves."

That word. *Love.* I don't flinch when he says it, because I know it's true. She's not *ours* yet. Not completely. But she will be. And until that day comes, we'll bleed for her. We'll burn the world for her. And we'll vanquish every single one of her ghosts.

Niko steps forward next, quiet as always. No theatrics. No speeches. He just grabs a branding iron and steps towards him with that cold, surgical calm that makes him the scariest one in the room.

The asshole lifts his head, face bloodied, lips trembling. "Please…"

"No." Niko says simply and slams the red-hot iron into his chest.

The smell of seared flesh and charred hair fills the room as the mark hisses against his skin. He thrashes, convulses, but there's nowhere for him to go. There's no hesitation in Niko's movements. No mercy. Just clean, efficient cruelty.

Rome steps forward with a pair of medical gloves and a tray Ezra left out earlier filled with scalpels, clamps, and bone spreaders. The kind of shit you'd find in a trauma ward. Rome selects a scalpel with a narrow tip, then crouches beside the bastard's right leg.

"Hold him," he says quietly.

Tristan obliges, and the asshole shakes again.

"Wha- what are you doing?" the man stammers, words slurring through pain and blood.

Rome doesn't answer. He makes a small incision just below the kneecap. Then another. And another.

He's flaying skin now. Slow, controlled, and clinical. Peeling it back like layers of something rotten. There's no anger in his expression, just focus.

"This is what it feels like," he says, voice low. "To be exposed. To have someone strip you down and decide what parts of you are worth keeping."

The man sobs. Rome doesn't flinch. He just continues. Steady. Detached. A surgeon dismantling something he never considered human. When the tendon twitches beneath the steel, he finally sets the scalpel down.

"You made her feel powerless," he says. "So now you don't get to feel human."

Then he peels off the gloves and backs away without a word.

Ezra watches from the corner, arms folded, eyes sharp. He's the conductor of this fucked-up symphony. Every tool here has a story. Every scream, a purpose.

Cyrus paces like a caged beast, tension vibrating off of him. And when he finally steps forward, he doesn't waste time. Just grabs the bolt cutters and stalks toward his fingers.

"S... start with the thumbs," Tristan offers, smirking from across the room. "Since the fucker likes to text so much."

The pop is sickening. The scream? Worse. But it's nothing compared to what she lived through.

So we take turns. Each of us pushing harder than the last. Because pain like this shouldn't be clean. It should stain. And it should come from *all* of us. A shared reckoning for the bastard who shattered her.

THIRTY-NINE

VIOLET

STEVIE AND ATLAS WALK ME UP TO THE GUESTHOUSE, BUT THEY don't hover. They don't ask if I'm okay. They don't need to. Because I think, they finally see it.

Not just the pain I carried. Not just the cracks in my voice or the scars on my skin. But the strength that came after.

I didn't kill him. But I didn't have to. I looked my monster in the eye and I walked away before he could take anything else from me. That was *my* choice. And whatever happens to him in Ezra's basement is none of my concern.

———

THE GUESTHOUSE IS BEAUTIFUL. Stevie designed it, so of course every detail feels intentional. The floors are warm-toned hardwood, the kind that don't creak under bare feet. The walls are a soft, dusty sage. There's a window seat tucked in the corner of the living room, and a line of floor-to-ceiling shelves filled with all of my favorite books. Romance. True crime. Even the manga collection I thought I lost in the move.

There are scented candles by the tub, a diffuser on the dresser, and a woven blanket in my favorite shade of lavender draped perfectly at the foot of the bed. It's peaceful. Cozy. Seriously cute. I can feel how carefully she built this place to make me feel like I belong.

And I do. Or... I should. But somehow, it still doesn't feel like mine. It's not comfort or beauty that's missing. It's *them*. The noise. The chaos.

Niko, always adjusting the thermostat too low and pretending it wasn't on purpose. Dallas, sprawling across the entire couch like he owned the place. Rome, moving through a room without touching anything, yet still taking up all the space.

This place is perfect. But I miss the mess, the presence. The feeling of being seen, even when I didn't want to be.

I sit on the bed, arms wrapped around my knees, and let the silence settle. It doesn't crawl across the floor like it used to. Doesn't strangle. Doesn't bite. It just exists. Soft and still.

You're safe now, I remind myself. *This is your home.* And yet, all I can think about is the one I left behind.

The clack of Rome's keyboard in the office. The ghost of Niko's cologne in the cushions. Dallas humming off-key while he cooked pancakes with too much syrup and not enough patience.

Their place was chaotic. Claustrophobic. A mess of mismatched mugs and weapons stashed in drawers. But it felt like home.

———

I DON'T SLEEP MUCH. But I don't dream either. Which feels like a win, all things considered.

By morning, I'm craving something familiar. So I pad into the main house with the half-formed idea of making breakfast for everyone. I step into the kitchen and find that someone's already beaten me to it.

Marta, their private chef, greets me with a smile.

"Good Morning Miss Alex," she says warmly. "Your sister and the boys are probably still sleeping, but I wanted to make sure you had something fresh to eat on your first day home."

She hands me a plate stacked with avocado toast, bacon and perfectly crisp hash browns. It smells delicious. Tastes even better. But it feels like someone else's version of home. Perfectly plated. Perfectly seasoned. But not mine.

I sit at the dining room table and eat in silence. There's no sarcastic comment from Rome about carbs. No gentle glance from Niko across the table. And no Dallas dramatically dropping three plates of food in front of me like he's worried I'm wasting away. Just me, a fork, and a meal I didn't ask for.

God, I miss them. And I *hate* that I do.

Stevie walks into the dining room a few minutes later, in leggings and a messy bun, holding a cup of coffee like it's the only thing keeping her upright. She takes the seat across from me and studies me for a long, quiet moment.

"Sleep okay?" she asks.

I nod.

She studies me for a moment. "You alright?"

I poke at my hash browns. "I will be."

She nods. "Can I ask you something?"

I glance up.

She hesitates for a second. "How did you feel about the guys?"

The question hits harder than I expect. I thought I'd moved past it. I thought I'd shut that door, but the ache in my chest says otherwise.

"I don't know," I murmur, stabbing at my toast. "It doesn't matter how I felt. It was all a lie anyway."

Stevie doesn't argue. She just sips her coffee.

"You should know…" she says gently, setting her cup down. "They sent the money back."

I freeze and look up to search her eyes. "What?"

"The night I confronted them," she says. "As soon as I left the building, they wired it back. Every cent. And they cancelled the exclusivity contract with us."

I stare at her.

"That doesn't mean I should forgive them," I whisper.

"No," she agrees softly. "It doesn't."

She pauses.

"But it is something to think about."

She leans forward, her voice steady, warm. "Whatever you decide… I trust you, Alex. You don't need anyone's permission. Not mine. Not theirs. You've already proven you're more than capable of standing on your own."

My throat tightens. I look down at my plate, blinking once. Then, I nod. For the first time in years I get to decide what comes next.

FORTY

NIKO

THREE MONTHS LATER

DR. KIM NEVER ASKS WHAT I'M THINKING. HE JUST WAITS. IT WAS annoying at first. The silence. The way he stares at me like he already knows and is just waiting for me to spill it. But after six sessions, I've figured out he's not trying to trap me. He just understands that I'm the type of man who will only speak when I'm ready to.

"I used to like the dark," I tell him, eyeing the corner of his chair. "It made things simpler. Easier to disappear. Safer."

He nods, waiting.

"It changed after a job. A kid was involved. Wasn't supposed to be. Everyone said the house would be empty." I pause. My throat tightens. "It wasn't."

Dr. Kim doesn't react. Just keeps listening.

"I found him in a closet. Hiding behind coats. Holding a stuffed lion covered in blood. He couldn't have been older than four."

The room's too quiet. It always is when I talk about this. I don't explain how his eyes were green like Violet's. I don't explain the way I froze. Or how I lied to keep him hidden. Or how I sat there and watched my boss drag him out.

I just say the only part I haven't said out loud yet.

"I didn't stop it."

There's a long pause.

Dr. Kim leans forward slightly. "You were a soldier. Under command. That doesn't make it okay, but-"

"No. It doesn't." I say, finally meeting his eyes. "He begged me for help, and I just sat there. So now... every time the lights go out, I see him. I see what I let happen. And I remember I didn't save him."

There's a long silence. Then I say the part I never thought I'd say.

"I did the same thing with Violet. I shut down. Her sister was pressing us, wanting to know what she meant to us. Vi was in the hallway listening, and I said nothing, even though I already knew how I felt about her."

"And how do you feel about her?

"Until Vi..." I pause, trying to find the right words. "I didn't think anyone could look at me and see anything but the worst parts. And I didn't give a damn if they did."

It's quiet for a long moment. My throat feels scraped raw, but the words keep coming.

"She makes me want to be... better. Not for me. For her. So when it matters, when it *really* matters, she knows I'll be there."

———

WHEN I GET BACK to the apartment, Ollie rushes up to greet me. Tongue out. Tail wagging. Dallas is on the couch, flipping through channels. Rome's in the kitchen with a glass of something brown and expensive.

Rome nods toward me. "Therapy?"

I nod back. "Yeah."

He lifts his glass slightly, like a quiet show of respect, then sips.

Dallas speaks without looking up. "I saw her this morning."

My spine straightens. "Where?"

He shrugs. "Little bakery downtown. She was working. Looked good. Happy."

Rome leans against the counter, arms crossed. "Stevie said she moved out of the guesthouse two weeks ago. Got her own place and everything."

Dallas tosses the remote onto the couch cushion beside him. "I didn't go in. Just... watched her through the window."

The silence turns sharp. Thick with things we'll never say out loud.

Finally, I ask, "What's the name of the bakery?"

Dallas glances at me. "Why?"

I don't answer, because I don't have a good one.

Dallas sighs, then tells me.

I nod once and say nothing else.

———

THE FIRST NIGHT I show up outside of the bakery, she flinches. Not visibly. Not in a way most people would catch. But I'm not most people and she's not just anyone.

She's got her keys looped around her fingers, her phone tucked under her arm, and her eyes are scanning the street like she's memorizing the shadows.

When she sees me, standing on the sidewalk, hands in my pockets, she stills for half a second. I don't say anything. I just fall into step beside her as she makes the walk from the back door of the bakery to the lot where her car is parked.

Three minutes. That's all I get. I don't ask her how she's been and she doesn't ask me why I'm there.

She just unlocks her car, gets in, and drives away. I stay until her taillights disappear. Then I go home.

It becomes a thing after that. Every night, closing time. Same corner of the lot. Same three-minute walk.

She never says much. Sometimes she nods. Sometimes she just looks at me like she's trying to solve a puzzle she isn't sure she wants the answer to. But she lets me walk her. Every time.

It's not about safety. *Not really.* The neighborhood is quiet. There are cameras, streetlights, and the police constantly patrol the area. It's about showing up for her, even when she doesn't ask, *especially* when she doesn't ask.

Some nights are harder than others. The dark still messes with my head. But I show up anyway. Because she's worth it. She's worth everything.

One night she turns to me, halfway through the walk, and says, "You don't have to do this, you know…"

I shrug. "I know."

She studies me for a second. "Then why do you?"

I hesitate.

Then say the only thing that feels true. "Because I want to."

That's it. No conditions. No expectations.

She nods, then unlocks her car. And this time she doesn't leave right away.She sits there in the driver's seat, engine off, watching me through the mirror like she's trying to decide something. Then she reaches across the console and pops the passenger lock.

I hesitate. It's new. *Different.* I open the door and slide in. The car smells like her. Like vanilla and and sugar and warmth. She keeps her hands on the wheel and stares out the window.

"You seem… different." She says quietly.

I lean back, watching her profile in the dim glow from the parking lot light.

"I'm finally dealing with all the shit in my head." I say, nodding. "Started going to therapy."

Her eyes flick to me. "That's good. Has it been helping?"

"I think so." I pause, tapping my fingers against my knees. "It's been hard, but I like doing the work."

She bites her lip, eyes still locked on the windshield. "Is that why you've been showing up here at night? Some sort of exposure therapy for the dark?"

"It's part of it," I admit.

She hesitates, fingers brushing over the stitching on the steering wheel.

"What's the other part?" She asks softly.

I glance at her. "You really want to know?"

She nods.

I close my eyes, and allow myself to be pulled back into the memory.

"Before I met Rome, I was involved in a gang that dealt with some nefarious shit. Violent assaults, extortion, assassinations. I was young, naïve, and eager to please. On this particular night, my crew was assigned a hit job. It was supposed to be clean. A rival gang leader and a few of his soldiers. We were told his family was gone for the weekend. Everyone was sure of it. *I* was sure of it."

Her hands tighten on the wheel, but she doesn't interrupt.

"Then I heard it. A kid crying. Muffled, somewhere in the drywall. I followed it to a closet, found a panel half-hidden behind some coats. He couldn't have been older than four. He was curled up with a stuffed lion soaked in someone else's blood."

Her breath hitches, but she stays quiet.

"When he saw me, he begged for his mom, and I didn't know what to do. Women and children had always been a hard line for me, but I should've made an exception then. I should've ended it for him so he wouldn't have to live through what came next." My jaw locks.

"But I couldn't do it. So I told him to be quiet, then I shut the panel, and waited in the dark for everyone else to clear out."

I lean forward, resting my elbows on my knees, as the memory scrapes against bones. "My boss came into the room for a final sweep and when I told him it was clear, he sensed the lie immediately. He shoved me out of the way, ripped the panel open, and dragged the kid out by his hair. As he was struggling, he looked right at me and begged me for help. And I just… watched."

The silence in the car is thick.

"I didn't intervene when he killed him. I didn't even cry. I just sat in the dark watching the life drain from his eyes. And now? Every time the lights go out, that's what I see. Not peace. Not quiet. Just that little boy and the reminder that I failed him."

I lift my head to meet her eyes. "That's why I'm here every night. Because I know I failed you, too. So, I'm going to do everything I can to prove that I'll never let you down again."

She holds my gaze, steady and unblinking, like she's trying to decide if she believes me. Then, slowly, she reaches into her glove box and pulls out a folded up piece of paper and tosses it into my lap.

I glance down.

It's a sketch. A delicate line work design of a crescent moon framed by a scatter of 9 tiny stars.

"I've got an appointment with Sean next Wednesday after work."

My fingers trace the edge of the paper, careful not to smudge it. It's beautiful. And more than that, it feels like a piece of her she's letting me see. She starts the engine, the low hum filling the quiet between us.

"You should come," she adds casually, but her eyes flick to me like the words matter more than she's letting on.

It takes me a second to answer.

"Yeah," I say, nodding my head. "I'll be there."

I fold the sketch carefully, set it back in her glove-box, and slip out of the car in the cool night air. The dark is still heavy, but it doesn't press as hard. Not when she's here with me.

FORTY-ONE

VIOLET

I'm halfway through my turkey club when I hear the click of nails on pavement. I look up and immediately groan.

"Ollie, no. Tell me he didn't…"

But there he is. Trotting around the corner of the café patio like a distinguished little gentleman on a mission. Ears alert, tail wagging, head high, like he's delivering royal correspondence.

Strapped to his back is a little khaki vest with bold black lettering stitched on the side: OPEN ME.

I drop my sandwich with a sigh. "Oh, that's low. Even for him."

I slide off the bench and crouch beside Ollie, who stops with theatrical flair and lifts one paw like he's offering a butler's tray.

"And you're his evil little accomplice," I mutter, scratching behind his ear.

He leans into the touch with a smug little huff, like he knows he's already won.

I glance toward the alley. The sidewalk. The street. No

sign of Dallas. There's a note tucked into the pocket on Ollie's vest, perfectly folded. *Ollie missed you. I didn't have the heart to tell him no.*

I snort. "Your papa's a manipulative bastard."

Ollie tilts his head like he agrees. Then I scratch under his chin and whisper, "He knows I can't resist this face."

———

EVERY DAY AFTER THAT, Ollie shows up. Same time. Same little vest. Same look on his face like, *"Ma'am, your special delivery has arrived."*

It's criminally effective. Sometimes it's a gift card to my favorite milk tea place across town. The one I once joked was my "emotional support sugar." Sometimes it's a dumb little note in Dallas' handwriting: *I've thought about it and San is my bias. Dimple gang!* Or: *Ollie thinks you like him better than me now. The little shit won't stop bragging about getting to hang out with you all the time.*

He never waits around. Never tries to talk, just sends Ollie to hang out with me during my lunch break and then vanishes like some emotionally intelligent ghost of situationship's past.

Until one day, I open the little pocket and concert tickets slip out. Three of them. Front row. Center stage. To the Stray Kids concert I once told him I'd trade a kidney to go to.

I stare at them for a full minute like they're going to self-destruct. Three tickets. Of course. Not two. Not four. *Three.* The subtlety would be infuriating if it wasn't so him.

A quiet *'maybe'*, a gentle *'if you want'* tucked between card stock. I sit with it for a while. Then I text Stevie.

———

THE CONCERT IS EPIC. Pyrotechnics. Lights. Fog. People sobbing with joy. Someone behind me screaming like the guys just proposed marriage to her. I should be euphoric.

But when the first slow song starts and I glance over to see Stevie wrapped in Ezra's arms, with his chin resting on her shoulder like it's his favorite place on earth, my chest twists.

I want that. I want the guy who sends Ollie in a tactical vest like it's a covert op for Operation: Win Back Girl. The one who never asked for anything. The one who was always there for me, even when I did everything I could to push him away. I pull out my phone before I can overthink it.

> I wish you were here.

My thumb hovers over the message, heart stuttering, then... I hit send. The response comes instantly.

> I was hoping you'd say that.

I look around, and there he is. Walking down the aisle like this is the most normal thing in the world. A ticket in one hand. The other stuffed in his jacket pocket. That stupid, hopeful grin barely hidden behind his dimples.

He reaches me and doesn't say a word. Just holds out his hand. I take it. His fingers wrap around mine, warm, steady, familiar.

We don't kiss, we don't talk, we just stand there hand in hand. In the glow of music and lights that make this moment feel like a new beginning.

FORTY-TWO

ROME

THE FIRST TIME I SEE HER NAME AGAIN, IT'S ON A MAINTENANCE report. Unit 5C. Intercom's shorting out. Heater's dead. The light in front of her door is flickering.

The building's in decent shape overall. Same architecture firm that designed ours. Same clean lines, same minimalist finishes. I remember thinking she probably picked it for that reason, because it felt familiar without feeling like us.

I don't know why I even looked at the report. But I did, over and over. Until I memorized every fault in her damn floor plan. Then I called my broker and bought the building. I said it was for logistical reasons. The old landlord was cutting corners, security was sloppy, and buying it would give me access to backend feeds.

No one questioned it. Because I'm methodical. Controlled. The kind of man who plans ten steps ahead. But the truth? *She's there.* And I'm not done taking care of her, even if she never opens the door for me again.

———

As soon as I get the keys, things start to change in Unit 5C. The heat comes back on. The intercom clicks into perfect clarity. The hallway light gets replaced with a warm-dim fixture that won't hurt her eyes in the morning.

She emails the management office. Says thank you and tries to confirm that her rent cleared. They say they'll look into it. But they never do, because I told them not to.

Every check she writes? I intercept. I pay it for her, quietly, so she never has to know. Because love doesn't always look like declarations. Sometimes it looks like four sturdy walls and a lease she never has to worry about.

———

The donuts come next. I send the same box to the lobby every morning, timed for when she heads out for work. Twelve assorted. With her favorite kind always on top. Pink with sprinkles. That one's hers. The rest? They go fast.

Building staff knows the drill. She gets first pick, and nobody touches the box until she walks past the lobby desk. I told them once. Never had to say it again. It's stupid, *sentimental*, but she always said the pink ones tasted better. So now? She gets one. Every day. No matter what.

———

Violet doesn't know I own the place now. I never stop her in the hallway. Never say hi in the elevator. Never remind her I'm still breathing her name in every silent moment between meetings and missions.

But I watch her. From the live security feed in my office, I see her come out of the elevator and cross the lobby.

Her apron is tied in the back, her hair is up, and her shoulders are relaxed in a way they never used to be. She looks happy. *Genuinely* happy. And while it does sting to know she's moved forward without me, I'm glad she's doing so well. She deserves good things, even if I'm not one of them.

———

OVER THE NEXT FEW WEEKS, more changes come. Better security for the building, a late-night patrol circling the block, her favorite snacks stocked at the corner store.

Then one morning, I'm monitoring the street cameras when I see her pause outside of a vacant storefront at the end of the block. She peeks through the front window and presses a hand to the glass like she's measuring the space with her eyes. Then, she shakes her head and keeps walking.

She's only there for a couple of minutes, but it sticks with me. So I buy it and put it under a trust. It's hers. Even if she never takes it. Even if she never speaks to me again.

I don't love her for what I get back. I love her for who she is. She's the only person who's ever looked at me like I wasn't just sharp edges and silence. She saw something in me, and she stayed. So now it's my turn. To see her, to stay, even if it is in the background.

If all I ever get is the chance to make her life easier, that'll be enough. But if she ever wants more. I'll be ready.

FORTY-THREE

VIOLET

THE HALLWAY SMELLS LIKE VANILLA AND LAVENDER. NOT THE fake, overly sweet kind either. The soft, herbal version I used to keep diffusing in my old room. The one Rome always claimed gave him headaches until I caught him standing in my doorway breathing it in like it was his new favorite scent.

I pause and glance at the diffuser tucked discreetly into the corner of the hallway. New. Sleek. Blinking a faint blue light. That wasn't here last week.

Ever since the new management took over, things have… shifted. Repairs actually happen now. The heater doesn't scream when it kicks on. The hallway light became this golden glow that didn't fry my retinas at midnight. My packages stopped getting stolen. They even replaced my flimsy front door with a new soundproof one reinforced with steel. And then there's the donuts.

Every morning, like clockwork, there's a box of donuts waiting in the lobby. Always the good kind. Always fresh. It's dumb, but it weirdly improves my day when I open the box and see my favorite kind, pink sprinkle, waiting for me. I *might* be emotionally attached to the routine.

I remember the first time I reached for one; the front desk guy nearly tackled a guy for trying to cut in front of me to swipe it first.

"That one's hers," he'd said, stone-faced.

Like I was royalty, and that donut was a crown jewel. I didn't ask questions. Mostly because I wanted the damn donut and that guy was a jerk for trying to cut. But lately, things feel... off. Not bad. Just *personal* in a way I can't explain. Like the universe has been paying attention a little *too* well.

————

I'M HALFWAY through flipping open the lid to the donut box when a slip of paper flutters out. It lands face-up on the edge of the lobby counter. Smooth, white, heat-pressed ink still curling at the corners. A receipt.

I blink down at it and I swear I see the name Roman scribbled on the top of it, but before I'm able to get a real look at it, the front desk guy lunges forward and snatches it up.

"I'll take that." He says too quickly. "We need the receipts for accounting."

Right. Because a building that just shelled out for steel-reinforced doors totally needs to account for every box of donuts.

I narrow my eyes at his too-tight smile, but I don't say anything else. I just grab my donut and leave. But that nagging feeling sticks with me, like frosting on my fingers. Sweet. Sticky. Hard to ignore.

————

AN ENVELOPE SHOWS up at my door a week later. No knock.

No delivery notice. Sitting on the welcome mat like it appeared there overnight.

Manila. Unmarked, except for a single Post-it stuck to the front.

For when you're ready.

There's no signature attached. No name. I stare at it for a long time before opening it.

Inside is a set of keys, a folded copy of a property deed, and a proposed floor plan. It's a storefront. *The* storefront. The one I passed on the way to work a month ago, half-wondering what it would feel like to fill that space with sugar and light.

It was just a thought. A quiet, wishful thing. But this... this is real. The paper in my hand says it's mine.

———

STEVIE DOESN'T SAY anything when I call her and tell her to meet me at my place. She just shows up with two iced lattes in hand. We don't talk much on the drive. She doesn't ask questions, just rides shotgun while I hold the deed like it might disappear if I blink too hard.

The shop is bigger inside than it looks on the outside. But it's also warmer. The kind of place people stop in on their worst days and their best ones, too. Inside, it's *perfect.*

Not finished, not yet. But framed out and painted. There's even a swatch board on the counter with five paint chips in soft pinks and warm neutrals. The walls are a gentle cream. The trim, a muted green that reminds me of the guesthouse I stayed in at her place.

There's a shelf already installed behind the counter, and it's the exact size I once said I'd need for a display case in my imaginary cafe. I can't even remember who I said that to-

Except I can. *Rome.* He remembered.

I turn slowly, heart thudding. "Stevie... did Rome do this?"

She's already watching me. Arms crossed. Brow raised.

"I had nothing to do with it," she says innocently.

I narrow my eyes.

She sighs. "Okay. Maybe he asked me for a little decorating advice. Maybe."

"Maybe?"

She shrugs. "He sent me swatches. Wanted to get it right. Said it should feel like you."

I stare at the space around me. The muted pink swatches. The soft lighting. The quiet potential. It does. It feels like me, or at least, the 'me' I'm finally becoming.

My fingers grip around the edge of the countertop, steadying myself. "I haven't spoken to him in months. Why would he do this?"

Stevie doesn't answer right away. She crosses the room to stand beside me and wraps her arm over my shoulders.

"Because love doesn't stop even when it hurts."

I blink hard. Swallow harder.

"You've already forgiven Dallas and Niko. Why haven't you forgiven him?"

I don't know. Maybe because his betrayal stung the most.

I shake my head. "He can't just buy me a building and think that'll win me back."

Stevie smirks. "If you think that's the only thing he's done for you, you haven't been paying attention."

I knew it. The changes in my building. The uncleared rent checks. The donuts. It's all been Rome working in the background.

"He didn't do this to win you back, Al. He did it because he wants to take care of you, even if he has to do it from a distance."

He's still here, in all the ways I thought he wasn't.

I look down at the keys in my hand. Feel the weight of them settle in my palm. They're solid and *real*.

Maybe this life I've been dreaming of isn't just a dream anymore. Maybe it's a beginning. And maybe he's still a part of it. *Maybe they all are.*

FORTY-FOUR

DALLAS

I'M NOT SURE WHAT WAKES ME FIRST. THE SILENCE OR THE missing weight beside me. Ollie's usually curled up at the end of my bed like a living furnace, but tonight? My sheets are cold, my room is empty, and his snoring is eerily absent.

I sit up and blink blearily at the clock. 11:59 P.M. He's probably trying to break into the fridge again. The little bastard's gotten smart lately. He's even learned how to open his treat drawer.

I pull on a pair of shorts and pad into the hall, scratching the back of my neck, and see Rome stepping out of his room. He's barefoot with sweats slung low on his hips, and his face is tight like he woke up on high alert.

"Did you hear that?" He mutters.

"It's Ollie," I say, yawning. "He gets the munchies at weird hours."

Niko appears behind us, rubbing his eyes like a pissed-off vampire. "Tell your dog to stop fucking around in the kitchen while we're trying to sleep."

"You say that like I can control him." I mumble.

Rome shakes his head. "Did he get into the trash again?"

I shrug. "There's only one way to find out."

We round the corner together. Three half-awake shirtless men expecting to catch our dog mid trash panda mode. Instead, we find *Violet*. Standing in the center of the kitchen, like a fever dream none of us deserve.

Her long lavender hair spills down her back in loose waves and she's wearing a crisp white apron with *nothing else underneath it*. Smooth tan skin, soft curves, and one perfect pink bow tied at the small of her back like a fucking present.

There's a cake on the counter. Candles lit, flames flickering.

She smiles. Sweet. Sinful. *Deadly*.

Rome goes statue-still beside me. Niko swears under his breath and spins away like he got clipped by a truck. Me? I'm pretty sure my soul leaves my body.

She looks at us, eyes sparkling with mischief.

"It's officially my birthday," she says lightly, bending over to blow out the candles. "I think you guys owe me a present."

She swipes a finger through the frosting, brings it to her lips, and licks it off slowly. My mouth goes dry, and my eyes drag over every inch of her. She tilts her head, gaze cutting across all three of us with a mischievous edge.

"I figured if I wore something you *all* liked… I wouldn't have to choose just one of you."

There's a girl we'd burn the world for, wrapped in a bow, and not a single doubt left in our minds. *Happy fucking birthday to us.*

FORTY-FIVE

VIOLET

THERE'S A MOMENT AFTER I BLOW OUT THE CANDLES WHEN NO one moves. The three of them just stand there frozen in the hallway, like they've forgotten how to breathe.

Dallas stares like he's memorizing every inch of me. Rome looks like he's seconds from pinning me to the wall. And Niko's gaze is fire and shadow, flickering like he's trying to decide whether to worship me or destroy me.

I lick the frosting off my finger and lock my eyes on Dallas.

"I figured if I wore something you all liked…" I trail off, gaze flicking to Rome, then Niko. "I wouldn't have to choose just one of you."

The air crackles. Then Rome moves. He doesn't rush me this time. He stalks. Like a storm made of restraint worn too thin. He steps behind me, and his fingers graze the bow at the small of my back.

"You sure?" He asks, his voice is low, dangerous.

I nod. "I've never been more sure."

He tugs the ribbon loose and the apron flutters to the floor.

Dallas swears under his breath and crosses the room like gravity's pulling him. His hands are warm when they cup my jaw, and he kisses me with open-mouthed reverence.

"You're insane," he whispers, biting my bottom lip. "You know that, right?"

I smile. "But you love it."

Niko's the last to move. His steps are silent, measured. But when he steps up and presses a kiss to my shoulder, the feeling of his breath skittering across my skin makes my knees go weak.

Three men. All of them surrounding me like I'm something holy. Dallas cradles my face, kissing me deep and slow. Rome's hands skim my hips, dragging me back against him as his mouth finds the shell of my ear. Niko kneels in front of me, trailing kisses down my stomach. I moan when he bites the inside of my thigh.

"Fuck," Dallas growls, pulling back just enough to look me in the eye. "You have no idea what you do to us."

They don't ask me to pick. They just give me everything. Hands and mouths and soft curses against flushed skin.

Dallas lifts me onto the counter, and Rome steps between my legs, dragging a finger through the frosting on my birthday cake. He swipes it over my pussy and I yelp, jerking in surprise.

"What-"

"I figured," Rome mutters, voice like gravel and sin, "if I'm going to break every rule I've got for you…" He kneels down, lowering his head between my legs. "I might as well start with dessert."

And then he *eats*. Not delicately. Not gently. He *devours*. Frosting and flesh and every filthy inch of me. His tongue dips where I'm slick and needy. And I gasp, nearly sobbing when his mouth seals over my tiny bundle of nerves and he starts lapping at it.

My hands slap the counter, body shaking. "Oh, my-*fuck*-Rome."

He growls something I can't hear because I'm *already coming*. Back bowed, thighs trembling, crying out. I asked for a birthday wish and got handed divinity.

Dallas chuckles low against my shoulder. "Carbs, huh?"

"Shut up," Rome snarls, tongue still buried inside me.

Dallas drags a smear of frosting across my stomach. Then he leans in, licking a path to my ribs before circling my nipples with his tongue.

Niko smears a line of frosting down my thigh and chases it with his tongue.

I moan, head falling back. They don't rush, they don't fight, they *share*. My legs tremble. My body's slick with sugar and sweat and an aching, consuming heat that burns me alive.

I fall apart again with Niko's mouth between my thighs this time and Rome's hand at my throat. And again when Dallas slides into me, slow and thick, while Niko thrusts into my mouth.

"Come here," Rome growls, lifting me up in his arms.

I line up above him, my thighs already shaking, and lower myself slowly, inch by thick, perfect inch, until he's deep inside me.

My head drops. A whimper escapes.

Rome grits his teeth. "You feel like fucking heaven."

Then I feel another set of hands wrap around my hips.

Niko.

He kneels behind me, palms splayed on my thighs as he positions himself between them. His cock brushes against where I'm already stretched full, and I freeze. Only for a second, until I feel Dallas' mouth at my ear.

"You trust us, beautiful?"

I nod, breathless.

"Then let him in."

I lift my legs, resting them in the crook of Rome's elbows, exposing everything. Niko pushes in alongside Rome, and I swear I black out for a second. Too full. Too much. Too *good*.

Rome holds me still, arms anchoring me in place, while Niko thrusts in slow and steady. His rhythm builds until I'm shaking from the effort to hold it together.

"Fuck," Niko groans, forehead pressed to my spine. "You're taking us so good, pretty girl."

I can't speak. I can only feel the press of them, thick and overwhelming, moving in sync, sliding deeper until every part of me feels owned.

They take turns, they take me together, and we keep going until we're all completely spent and none of us can take anymore.

I lie between them on the kitchen floor, a hand in Dallas' hair, Niko's arm slung across my waist, and Rome pressed behind me with his hand on my chest. I've never felt more safe, never felt more seen, never felt more *loved*.

As sleep pulls me under, Dallas leans closer and murmurs against my throat, "Best birthday ever."

I shake my head with a smile. "Glad you enjoyed my present."

Rome huffs a laugh. "We should unwrap you again tomorrow."

I close my eyes, sinking into the safety of my men. "Tomorrow. The next day. And every day after that, as long as you'll have me."

"So, forever then?" Niko asks.

I smile, eyes still closed. "Yeah. Forever works for me."

EPILOGUE: PART 1

VIOLET

I used to think survival was the best I could hope for. Turns out, it's *this*. A glass case filled with handmade sweet and savory pastries. A line of hungry customers out the door. And the three gorgeous men willing to spend mornings slinging baked goods with me.

I wipe my hands on my apron and glance around the cafe. In the front window, Dallas flexes as he flips the "Grand Opening" sign. A group of teenage girls giggle as he waves like he's on a damn parade float.

"Stop flirting with minors," I call out.

He turns around with a grin. "I'm not flirting, I'm boosting brand visibility."

"You're gonna boost your way into a prison cell," Rome mumbles, cleaning the glass in front of the pastry case for the third time this hour.

"Should we be concerned," I whisper to Niko. "I swear I saw him wiped it down ten minutes ago."

Niko smirks and slides another tray of crème brûlée donuts onto the baker's rack. He's wearing black, of course, like this is a funeral and not the most exciting day of my life. But he scorched the tops of those donuts himself and I saw the way his mouth twitched when I said they looked perfect. Even if he won't admit it, he's proud. I am too.

Ollie trots across the tile, tail wagging like he owns the place. He's got a "Head of Security" bandana around his neck. He stops at a table with two older ladies and flops dramatically at their feet, earning immediate coos and crumbs.

Sugar & Snout is a dog-friendly cafe. That was nonnegotiable. I even put up a little sign at the front that says, *Well-behaved dogs welcome. Humans too, I guess.*

Ollie's the one who brings in most of the business, anyway.

——————

Two hours into our grand opening, the bell above the door jingles, and chaos walks in. Stevie and her guys: Atlas, Ezra, Tristan, and Cyrus, make a beeline for the front counter like they've been fasting for weeks.

Cyrus stops dead in front of the display case, eyes locked on the full line of ham and Gruyère croissants. I swear I see him tear up.

"It looks great, baby sis," Stevie says, her eyes sweeping across the café, slow and proud. "You really freaking did it."

I swallow, still not used to hearing things like that.

"Thanks. It still scares me, you know? Having something good. I keep thinking I'm going to mess it all up," I admit quietly.

"You won't." She leans across the counter and tucks a stray strand of hair behind my ear. "You were made for this."

My throat tightens, and I nod.

Behind her, Ezra is already reaching over a stranger's shoulder to steal a tart off their plate.

"S… seriously?" Tristan swats his hand away with a scowl.

Cyrus lets out a wheezing laugh. Atlas just sighs like he's accepted this is his life now.

"Sorry," Stevie says with a groan, massaging her temples. "They're animals."

She turns back to me. "Could we just get one of everything?"

I laugh and reach for a pastry box, the warmth settling back into my chest as I load it up for them.

"Do you ever get used to wrangling that many guys all at once?" I ask, sliding her the filled box.

"No," she deadpans, shaking her head. "Not at all. But at the same time… I wouldn't have it any other way."

I glance across the café at my own little family. Dallas is now behind the register, telling a customer their coffee comes with a smile, then flashing his dimples like it's a legally binding promise. Rome is refolding napkins that are already perfectly aligned, muttering under his breath like they're refusing to fall in line. Niko is leaning against the back wall, sipping his coffee and pretending like he's not sneaking treats to the golden retriever puppy waiting at his feet. And right in the middle of it all, Ollie is hopping up onto a chair with his snout creeping toward an unattended croissant like he wasn't just fed twenty minutes ago.

I look at them, at my mess, my peace, my people, and I feel something settle in my chest.

"I know exactly what you mean." I say, smiling at her.

A soft breeze slips in through the open front door, carrying the smell of sugar, espresso, and freshly baked goods.

Customers laugh. Stevie rolls her eyes at Ezra. Ollie finally steals the croissant. And for the first time in my life, I don't brace for the crash. I let myself enjoy it. Because I didn't just survive, I built something worth living for. And I'm never ever letting it go.

EPILOGUE: PART 2

VIOLET

We're exactly thirty-three minutes into the movie when Rome groans for the fourth time.

"This is a cartoon," he mutters, arms crossed like he's gearing up for war.

"It's an animated movie with incredible emotional depth," I say, stealing a handful of popcorn from Dallas' lap.

Niko tilts his head from the corner of the couch. "They're fighting demons… with choreography."

"That's the point," Dallas and I say in unison.

Rome sighs again, like he's hoping we'll feel sorry for him and turn it off.

Spoiler Alert: We won't.

"You agreed to movie night," Dallas says, shoving a pillow under his head. "That means democracy. You were outvoted."

Niko mumbles something under his breath. I don't catch all of it, but I'm pretty sure it alludes to emotional manipulation.

I sink deeper into the couch as the movie plays on with a

blanket tucked around my legs. Ollie is out cold, snoring between my feet like a weighted pillow with attitude. Rome is sitting rigidly at one end of the couch, jaw clenched, trying not to look interested, as he taps his feet to the music. And Niko is lounging against the armrest, hood up like that'll protect him from the heartbreak to come. It won't. Because we're almost there.

Dallas catches my eye and grins. I grin back. They have no idea what's about to hit them.And then it happens. Jinu steps in front of the Demon King's fire. He apologizes to Rumi for betraying her trust, and he gives her his soul. The light explodes. His body disappears into a plume of soft blue smoke and glitter. And Rumi stares in horror at the space he left behind.

There's a beat of silence. Then. *Sniff.* Rome shifts in his seat like it's suddenly too small. Niko presses his thumb to the corner of his eye, jaw tight. Dallas nudges my foot beneath the blanket. I bury my face in my sleeve to keep from laughing.

"You guys good?" I ask, voice laced with fake innocence.

"I'm fine," Rome says too fast, clearing his throat.

Niko doesn't even look over. "It's just... well animated."

"Right," I whisper. "Totally."

The rest of the movie plays on, and we all fall quiet as the credits roll, upbeat music swelling in the background. Ollie sighs deeply, shifting just enough to smother the remote under his chunky body.

Dallas reaches under him to fish out the remote, grumbling like it's a hostage negotiation. Rome finally settles back into the cushions, arms crossed, but he doesn't move away when I lean into him. And Niko grabs the remote and starts the movie over again without saying a word.

The room is warm and soft and cluttered with half-eaten snacks and mismatched socks and the quiet kind of peace that used to feel like a fantasy. My guys, pretending not to cry over an animated K-pop movie. Me, pretending not to love them even more for it.

This ridiculous, beautiful mess. It's ours. And this time, I don't feel like I have to earn it. I just get to keep it. *Forever.*

Want more from Jessa?
Signup for my free newsletter
to receive exclusive access & offers

Turn the page for a sneak peek of

I'LL
BE
THERE
FOR
YOU

JESSA HALLIWELL

I'LL BE THERE FOR YOU

PROLOGUE

DAHLIA

Age 17, Carnesville, Georgia

No one tells you what you're supposed to wear to your ex's murder trial.

I spent twenty minutes staring at my closet this morning. Agonizing over the choice before finally settling on a plain black sweater and a pair of dark jeans that I hoped would help keep me invisible. Kind of stupid in hindsight, considering it probably doesn't matter. Everyone in this town recognizes me by now.

I almost didn't show up today.

After testifying last month, I promised myself I'd never set foot in this town again. But the verdict is in and I need to hear it for myself. Need to know, beyond a shadow of a doubt, that he won't ever be able to hurt anyone else again.

The wooden bench creaks beneath me as I take a seat in one of the only open spots left in the courtroom. Dozens of eyes laser their focus on me and, as if on cue, the whispering starts.

Christian sits at the defense table like it's just another Tuesday for him. His posture is relaxed, his suit is pressed, and his golden-brown hair is styled perfectly, with not even a strand out of place. He looks normal. Sane even. Nothing like the monster he's proven himself to be.

"That's her." A woman behind me whispers. "The girlfriend."

Ex-girlfriend, I mentally correct, *not that it makes a difference to any of these people.*

"I still think she put him up to it." Another woman whispers back. "I know the family. He was a good boy until he met her."

Swallowing hard, I wrap my fingers around the edge of the bench beneath me and let my nails dig into the thick varnish to try to help ground myself.

I didn't put Christian up to anything. *I know I didn't.* But I can't help but feel the truth in what she's saying.

I may not have had any idea what he was planning, but I caused this. I was the catalyst that drove Christian to do what he did that night, and I deserve to carry as much of the blame as he does.

"I don't know how the hell she lives with herself." The first woman adds, letting hate radiate from every syllable.

The truth is I don't.

I breathe, I eat, and I sleep when I can. But I don't live. I just exist. And honestly, after everything that happened, I'm not sure I even deserve that.

"She doesn't care." A man hisses, not even bothering to lower his voice. "They were her parents, for God's sake, but that didn't matter to her."

At the mention of my parents, grief slams into me with such crushing force it nearly knocks the wind out of me. My head drops, and the tears that I've been desperately trying to rein in since I got here finally spill over.

Fuck.

I can't do this. I can't be here.

It's too hard. It's too much.

I shake my head, and my watery gaze drifts to the empty seats beside me. The ones Mom and Dad would be sitting in if it weren't for me. I can almost feel Dad's hand patting my knee, in that awkward, stoic way of his. Can almost hear Mom's lovingly teasing words in my ear.

Don't cry, Anak. Papangit ka.

Don't cry, daughter. You'll get ugly.

A sad smile spreads across my face.

God, I miss them.

And it's not just their presence that I miss most; it's all the little things. Their laughs. The ones that were too loud and way too infectious. Their food. No one, and I mean no one, can cook like my dad. Their love. It was never really expressed out loud, and honestly, I used to resent them for that, but now that I know what it feels like to be without it, I know I felt it in everything they did for me. *Every fucking thing.*

More unwelcome tears slide down my cheeks, and I swipe them away with the sleeve of my sweater and try to pull myself together.

Stop it. Stop crying right now. You need to be strong, if not for yourself, for them.

Blowing out a shaky breath, I blink back my tears and force my head up, only to find Christian turned in his seat, staring at me.

I've seen him a handful of times over the course of the thirteen-month trial, but looking him in the eye hasn't gotten any easier. It's like my brain still hasn't fully accepted that the monster sitting on trial in front of me is the same boy I fell in love with freshman year.

"I love you." Christian mouths, the words, silent, yet somehow clear as day.

And I should have never loved you. I think to myself, fixing my eyes on the weathered wainscoting behind him.

Christian glares at me, and after a few tense seconds, he sighs and finally turns back around in his seat.

Seconds later, the bailiff clears his throat, and the courtroom dulls to a hushed silence. "All rise." He says. "The Honorable Judge Walker is now entering the courtroom."

Benches groan and metal chair legs screech across the scuffed terrazzo floor. A door near the front of the room opens, and the judge steps in with his black robe billowing behind him. He takes his seat, and the bailiff orders the rest of us to do the same.

The judge places his wiry glasses on the tip of his bulbous nose and looks at the jury. "Members of the jury, have you reached a verdict?"

A bald man in his late forties rises from his seat in the jury box. "We have, Your Honor. On two counts of murder in the first degree, we find the defendant Christian Sanders... *guilty.*"

I don't hear the rest of the verdict.

I'm too busy trying to remember how to breathe.

The courtroom erupts in chaos around me, with everything ranging from screams to cheers to full-on sobs echoing through the tiny courtroom. A sharp wail rises above the rest, Christian's mother, and the sound of her agony is so palpable, just hearing it brings fresh tears to my eyes.

I drag my gaze over to Christian, but he doesn't even look fazed. He's still sitting at the defense table with his jaw flexed and an otherwise blank expression on his face. Two officers approach him with cuffs in hand, and as his stone-faced lawyers rise from their seats, Christian turns around to face the courtroom.

"I did this for us, Dollface!" He yells, looking directly at me. His voice is laced with so much conviction it makes my whole body lock up. "I fucking love you. I always have, and I always will."

A murmur ripples through the crowd as accusing glances dart my way. If people didn't notice I was here before, they do now.

People shout over one another as reporters scramble toward me, and cameras flash like strobe lights from every direction.

I need to get the hell out of here. I need to leave right now before it gets worse. But the exit feels miles away, and the thought of turning around to face the crowd is nauseating.

A hand touches my shoulder, and I flinch, jerking violently before I can stop myself. It's the bailiff.

"Miss, let's have you exit through the side door."

I'm numb. So fucking numb. But I stand up from my seat and follow him, keeping my eyes fixed on the floor.

Mom.

Dad.

They didn't deserve this. They were innocent. I was the guilty one. I should've heeded the signs. I should've known what was coming. I should've fucking stopped him. But I was too stupid. I was too *in love*. And I have no one to blame but myself for that.

I used to think love was the answer to everything. That it was this pure and enviable thing that I could only dream of having. But now I see love for what it truly is.

A disease.

A sickness that infects your brain and destroys everything in its path. And my love just might be the most insidious strain of all.

It turned Christian into a monster.

It turned me into an idiot.

And it stole every single person I've ever cared about.

My love fucking destroyed me.

And I'll never let it infect anyone else again.

I'LL BE THERE FOR YOU

CHAPTER ONE

DAHLIA

Age 27, San Francisco, California

MALE BONDING IS WEIRD AS FUCK.

I stare at Josh and watch him take another long swig of his beer as his friends Dane, Nate, and Michael, erupt in laughter at his expense. They're laughing so loud I can literally feel it in my bones, which is kind of impressive considering I'm sitting on the opposite side of the booth and there's at least a dozen flatscreens blasting a cacophony of sport sounds at us.

It's obvious Josh hates the ridicule. He's clenching his fist and his ears are turning redder and redder as their jeering stretches on, but instead of telling them to stop or trying to change the subject, he just sits there and takes it.

It's almost hard to watch.

Maybe he's a masochist?

Or has some kind of humiliation kink?

Either would be pretty surprising considering we've been on five dates and he seems as vanilla as my favorite kind of Coke.

Not that there's anything wrong with vanilla. It's comforting. Nice. Safe.

Ugh, why does it feel like I'm describing a cozy cottage near a lake?

We haven't even had sex yet, but I have a feeling there will be little to no orgasms in my near future.

Don't get me wrong, Josh is handsome. He has this sort of clean-cut, all-American look to him, with his sandy brownish-blonde hair and kind blue eyes that you could easily get lost in. Is he exactly my type? No. But that's probably a good thing.

As if summoned by my pessimistic thoughts, Josh reaches under the table and gives my hand a gentle squeeze.

God, I need to be nicer to him. Josh is a nice guy and could actually be good-for-me. Who cares if he has terrible friends and the spine of a jellyfish? At least I know he'd never hurt me. He may not be what I want, but he could be what I need. And after everything I've been through, that has to count for something.

Besides, the man practically worships the ground I walk on and has been bending over backwards to make tonight happen. I rarely do the whole "meet the friends" thing, but when he showed up at Better Than Fiction unannounced and practically begged me to come out with him and his friends after work, I didn't have the heart to tell him no.

Apparently, they've been giving him shit about making me up and that me "always being busy at my bookstore" was just an excuse to cover up his obvious lie.

While running the shop does keep me busy, I'd be lying if I said that was the only reason I've been avoiding them.

The thing is, meeting friends makes things between us more serious. And the minute things get serious, the next expectation is love.

What I feel for Josh isn't anywhere close to love, and for me, it never will be.

He says he's okay with that. That he's willing to take whatever I'll give him. But that's what everyone says before they catch feelings and the reality of my damage sinks in.

I stir my pineapple vodka and watch the four of them, feeling disconnected from the whole scene.

Josh's friends weren't very attractive to begin with, but they're all just a touch uglier when they laugh like this. It's like the features that looked a little wonky on them before, are even more pronounced now.

Dane's beady eyes are beadier.

Nate's scrunched up nose is scrunchier.

And Michael's veiny forehead is veinier.

I stop stirring my drink and freeze.

Shit.

Do I look uglier when I laugh, too?

Goddamnit, now I need to check.

After making sure they're all still deeply enthralled in their jabbing contest, I flip my compact open under the table and stare at my reflection as I discretely mimic my laughing faces.

Okay, the nose is still nosing…

The teeth are still teething…

The eyes are still eyeing…

"Dahlia… what are you doing?"

The sound of Josh's voice startles the hell out of me. I snap my compact shut and look up to find him and his friends staring.

"Huh?" I reply automatically, despite the fact that I definitely heard him the first time.

Josh furrows his brow. "I asked what you were doing."

I swallow and my eyes ping-pong between him and his three friends.

Fuck, I knew coming out with them was a bad idea.

"I uhh… thought I had something stuck in my teeth." I say, pointing vaguely to my mouth.

Josh cocks his head at me, as do his friends, and warmth rushes up neck. I try to break the awkwardness with a laugh, but Josh doesn't even crack a smile. He just stares at me.

"Beautiful and funny." Nate says, squeezing Josh's shoulder. "No wonder this poor fuck thinks you're the love of his life."

The forced smile on my face dies immediately.

What?

Why the hell would he think that?

I look around the table, and Josh's eyes cut to me so fast it makes my stomach flip. I take in Josh's expression. He doesn't look embarrassed or angry. He looks *guilty.*

The truth punches me in the face.

Josh thinks I'm the love of his life. We've only been on five dates and he's already there. We haven't even had sex yet, and he's already there.

This can't be happening.

I plaster a smile on my face and take another sip of my drink, hoping the act of normalcy will be enough to stop them from scrutinizing my reaction. It works, and their conversations continue, but it doesn't stop the panic from churning in my stomach.

I grip the edge of my seat to try to ground myself, but it's no use. And the longer I sit here, the more claustrophobic I feel. I can't breathe. I need to get out of here. *Now.*

My legs feel like they're filled with concrete as I slide out of the booth, but I force them to move, anyway.

"Doll?" Josh calls out, noticing my departure. "Where are you going?"

"Bathroom." I chirp back. He's trying to search my face, but I can't bring myself to look him in the eye.

"Let me show you where it is." He offers, already sliding his body across the pleather seat.

"I'll find it." I reply, waving a hand at him. "Stay with your friends."

Josh pauses mid-stand, and his brow furrows. "Are you sure—"

"Yeah. I'll be back."

Josh frowns as he studies my face, and I can see the muscles working in his throat. He doesn't say anything, probably because his friends are paying attention now, but his eyes are begging me not to leave. He body looks filled with tension as he watches my retreat, and I can tell it's taking all of his willpower not to chase after me.

One of his friends, Michael, I think, breaks the tension by coughing "simp" under his breath, and the others laugh again.

Josh doesn't join them. Instead, his eyes stay on me. I can feel them burning into my back, even after I turn and walk away.

I'LL BE THERE FOR YOU

CHAPTER TWO

DAHLIA

THE HALLWAY I'M WALKING DOWN IS NARROW AND DIMLY LIT, lined with dozens of autographed photos of celebrities I vaguely recognize. I glance at each one as I pass to help distract myself, but after a while, it starts to feel dizzying, so I give up and focus on the floor instead.

Releasing a long sigh, I massage my temples and try my hardest to rub the memory of Josh's pathetic puppy-dog face from my head.

God, I knew coming here was a mistake.

Five dates.

Five freaking dates.

That has to be a new record for me.

On the bright side, it's still early enough to end things without too much fallout, so I guess there's that.

I let out a sigh.

I honestly don't even know why I bother dating anymore. I'm fundamentally incapable of giving people the one thing they're really after. And contrary to popular belief, it isn't just sex that men want most, it's love, adoration, and attachment.

Sex, I can do. Sex is simpler. Sex can happen without feelings ever needing to be involved. But all of that other stuff cannot, and I can't keep setting myself up for failure like this.

Maybe I just need to create a Tinder account and be completely blunt about what I can handle to save everyone the trouble.

Hey, I'm Dahlia Delacruz. I'm 27 and my hobbies include reading, watching movies, and running away at the first sign of emotional attachment. Wanna bang?

A harsh laugh spills from my lips.

Yeah, that's a great way to attract a sociopath.

The hallway curves to the right, and I follow it, expecting to finally find the restroom, but instead, I land in some kind of storage hallway. There's a long line of metal shelves filled with various food packaging supplies, and a bunch of liquor boxes piled against the wall.

I'm probably not supposed to be back here, and I definitely took a wrong turn somewhere, but I'm not even mad about it. The farther away from Josh and his friends, the better.

The heels of my boots click softly against the linoleum floor as I wander farther down the hall, biding my time. And before long, I reach the end of the hallway. I'm about to turn around when my eyes catch on the emergency exit. There's an empty milk crate wedged against the door, holding it open just enough to let a sliver of the back alley peek through.

God, yes.

Exactly what I need. An escape route I can take without having to explain myself to anyone. No awkward conversations. No evading questions. No public displays of emotion.

Before I can overthink it, I shove the door open and step outside.

The alley behind the sports bar is nearly pitch black, save for the few scattered streetlights, casting dim pools of yellow on the rain-slicked pavement.

I walk along the side of the building, or at least I think I do, but I can barely see anything beyond the silhouette of a few dumpsters and parked cars ahead of me. It's so disorienting. The alley keeps branching off into smaller, darker paths, and it feels longer and more twisted than it should.

Jesus, it's cold tonight, I think to myself, wrapping my bare arms across my chest for warmth. *And of course, I left my jacket in the car.*

Fuck, I think I'm lost.

I fish through my purse for my phone, and just as I'm about to pull up the navigation app, the sound of voices cuts through the silence.

Shit. Someone else is out here.

Chilling sounds of laughter echo in the wind and are swiftly followed by grunts of what I can only assume is pain.

Fuck. Someone's in trouble.

This isn't your problem. I think, trying to reason with myself. *No one would judge you if you walked away right now.*

I would judge me, I argue back, *I would blame myself for not at least trying to help.*

I follow the sounds and do everything I can to stay as hidden as possible.

Maybe it's a couple of friends play fighting. Maybe it's some drunk asshole laughing at his own stupidity. Maybe it's nothing. All of my maybes go to shit when I round the corner and find a brutal scene playing out before me.

Four men, each one bigger than the last, are attacking someone on the ground. Their feet rise and fall in a sickening rhythm, and the man's body rocks with every blow.

Jesus. They're going to kill him.

My instincts scream at me to run, to get the hell out of here before they notice me. But with each crack of bone on bone, my resolve grows. I can't just stand here and let them kill him. I won't. No one deserves to have their life violently stolen from them like that. No one.

"Stop it!" I shout, the words tearing out of me before I can think better of them.

All four heads snap in my direction, and their eyes narrow like predators spotting prey.

The shortest of them laughs. "You lost, little girl?"

I scan my surroundings, taking in the four massive figures, the dim lighting, and the lack of any clear escape route.

Four against one. Not great odds in general, but especially shitty when the one has heeled boots on. *Fuck.*

Running isn't an option. I have the pocket-knife Fallon got me hidden in my sock, but I've never even used it, and I know it won't be enough to scare them off. My mind races.

"Look, I-I don't want any trouble." I stutter, stepping back.

The biggest one, with a nasty scar across his cheek, advances. "Then you shouldn't have come looking for it, sweetheart."

I take another step back, eyes darting to the man on the ground. His eyes are closed, but his chest is still moving up and down. Good, he's still breathing. I silently will him to get up and run. But he just lies there. *Shit.*

"Stay back," I warn, holding my phone up like a shield, "Or I swear to God, I'll call the cops."

"Oh no, guys," the big one mocks, "guess we better leave her alone."

The others laugh as they follow behind him. My stomach twists as their smug smiles widen. This is bad. This is really fucking bad.

The big one comes at me first, cornering me against the side of a building. He lunges for me and, without hesitation, I duck down, yank the pocket knife from my boot, and pop back up, slashing wildly.

The blade catches the side of his face and carves through his skin in a jagged slice. The wet sound he makes as his hands fly up to his bleeding face makes my stomach churn.

Shock ripples through his friends, and their laughter dies immediately. Then, without warning, they attack.

The man closest to him tries to grab me, but I twist out of his hold and use my shoulder to slam into his chest, hard. He stumbles back a step, more caught off guard than hurt, but it's enough to give me a second to prepare myself.

Another man comes for me, faster than the other two, and I wildly swing the knife in his direction. He pulls back just in time, leaving the blade to slice the air where his stomach had been a second ago.

"She fucking stabbed him!" He yells, looking between his bleeding friend and the knife in my hand.

The last man stares at me and goes to reach for the gun at his waistband. The sight of it sends pure terror ricocheting through my body. If he grabs that gun, I'm dead.

I charge him without thinking, my knife slicing at him in shallow, messy strikes. He curses at me and slams his elbow into my back, knocking the breath from my lungs and sending me tumbling forward.

As soon as I hit the ground, rough hands grab me from every direction. Ripping at anything they can get their hands on. Someone pries the knife from my grip, and before I even realize what's happening, I'm forced back on my feet, and a thick arm is wrapping around my neck and crushing my throat.

Fuck.

I claw at the arm choking me, kicking wildly, but my feet barely scrape the pavement as he lifts me off the ground with terrifying ease.

"Kill that bitch, Rico!" One of them shouts, tending to the first man I stabbed. "Look what she did to Aldo!"

The arm around my neck squeezes harder, and my vision starts to blur at the edges. I try to head-butt his chin, but miss, and in return, he slams my face hard against the brick wall. White explodes behind my eyes.

"You have no idea who you're fucking with," he snarls, pressing his cracked lips to my ear.

I try to kick, to fight, to do something, but my body betrays me. He has me pinned against the brick wall, and my limbs are heavy and utterly useless.

I can't breathe. I can't fucking breathe.

A deafening bang rings out, and I flinch as the sound ricochets through my entire body. The arm around my neck loosens, and the weight pressing against me eases off.

I suck in a ragged breath as I turn to face them, my eyes narrowing at the puzzling scene. The four of them are just standing there, staring at each other with wide-eyed confusion.

What the hell is happening?

Another bang rings out, and the man who was just choking me jerks forward. Before I can even process what's happening, his face explodes, and he collapses to the ground. Another one sounds, then another, and another, and like a twisted version of "Down the Clown" the rest of the men collapse next to him. Their bodies land with sickening thumps, and I stare, transfixed on the glistening pools of blood stretching across the pavement beneath them.

I slowly look back up, and the sight in front of me makes me audibly gasp.

The man they were beating is now standing. He's tall, at least a foot or more above me. Maybe somewhere around 6'5 or 6'6. There's a gun in his hand and a gnarly gash above his brow. Blood streaks down the side of his face, sliding against the hollow of his cheeks before catching on the edge of his clenched jaw. He stares at me through the dark strands of hair hanging over his eyes, and I can't help but stare back.

He's stupidly pretty for a killer.

Full brows, dark eyes, and the kind of panty-melting bone structure you can stare at for hours. He has tattoos crawling up the side of his neck, half hidden by the collar of his white shirt, and despite the blood and the gun and the four bodies at his feet, he looks completely unfazed.

He takes a step towards me, and I flinch back, pressing myself harder into the brick. I'm trying to stay calm, but my body is acting purely on instinct. It's as if it can sense the danger I'm in and has shifted into pure self-preservation mode.

As he inches closer, his eyes stay on mine, then dip lower for a second too long, before lazily lifting back up.

I glance down at myself.

Shit.

One of the straps on my dress is torn, and the neckline is pulled down and stretched from where their hands grabbed at me. I didn't wear a bra today, and my breasts are almost completely exposed.

I jerk my arms up immediately, yanking the fabric back into place, and trying to cover myself as best I can. When I look back up, I find him watching.

The muscles in his jaw flex, and then he slides his gun into the waistband of his pants.

My grip tightens on the fabric as my brain scrambles, every instinct screaming at me all at once. *What is he doing?*

He starts to take off his jacket, and I freeze.

He's just as bad as they are, a voice in the back of my head whispers. *He's worse. You misread the situation. You saved a monster.*

He strips the jacket off, and I just stand there trembling, bracing for something I can't even force myself to think about. Then, without warning, he tosses it at me.

The jacket flies in my direction, and I barely manage to catch it before it falls to the ground. For a moment, I just stand there staring at the warm pile of burgundy fabric clenched in my hands.

"Put it on." He says, sounding almost annoyed.

I hesitate, only because my brain hasn't fully caught up to what's happening, then quickly throw it on.

The jacket is heavier than I expected, and as the warm fabric settles over my shoulders, heat seeps in almost immediately. It smells faintly of smoke and a warm, woody fragrance. Something subtle but unmistakably expensive. The feel of his jacket draped over me is grounding in a way that doesn't make sense.

My breathing calms down a little, and when I look up, he's watching me again.

He stares at me for a moment, studying my face, then, ever so slowly, he pulls his gun from his waistband, levels it at my head, and smirks as he says, "This is the part where you run."

CLICK HERE to get the full story

DEAR READER, YOU'RE THE SHIT.

Thank you for reading Violet's story! If you enjoyed it, please consider leaving a review or sharing it on social media. It's the easiest way to support Indie Authors like me, and your reviews make a huge impact.

It took me about three years to finally bring Twisted Violet to life, and I could not be happier with how it turned out.

While this is a spinoff of The Reapers Trilogy, I really wanted this story to feel like Violet's completely, so I pulled back on the action/violence (even though I love writing it haha) to really focus on her internal battles and her healing journey.

Violet is the polar opposite of her badass sister. She's soft, timid, and sweet. But I hope this story shows that strength comes in many forms and that no matter what you've been through, we're all deserving of love.

Thank you again for your support, and I can't wait to give you many more stories soon!

LOVESICK VILLAINS

Fear The Reapers
A Dark Mafia Reverse Harem Romance
A Lovesick Villains Trilogy: Book 1

Queen of The Reapers
A Dark Mafia Reverse Harem Romance
A Lovesick Villains Trilogy: Book 2

Wrath of The Reapers
A Dark Mafia Reverse Harem Romance
A Lovesick Villains Trilogy: Book 3

Twisted Violet
A Dark Reverse Harem Romance
A Lovesick Villains Standalone

ABOUT JESSA

Jessa Halliwell *is a Dark Romance Author who writes about angsty, torturous love mixed with a dash of danger. She loves writing romance only slightly more than she loves reading it. She's been known to binge read novels then spend the rest of the day sulking over the massive book hangover.*

Jessa resides in Northern California with her boyfriend and her sassy German Shepherd Mix named Nugget. When she isn't writing, you can find her obsessing over her skincare routine, drinking an unhealthy amount of hibiscus tea, or probably crying over a really good book.

Follow me on tiktok: @jessahalliwell
    Follow me on IG: @jessahalliwellauthor
    Join my Facebook Readers Groups: Jessa Halliwell's Lovesick Villains

www.ingramcontent.com/pod-product-compliance
Lightning Source LLC
Chambersburg PA
CBHW031156020726
47499CB00002B/388